A Choice for Claire

a novel by

AJ Harmon

First Print Edition, February 2015

Caution:

This book contains scenes of rape and domestic violence, and real life situations. Please be aware of the nature of this book. Ages 18 and over only.

Dedication

The notion that a writer sits alone day after day writing with no interaction with other human beings may be accurate for some writers, but not this girl! While it's true I write by myself, I am *never* alone.

To my P.A. Stefanie, I am so glad you are with me on this amazing experience. You take care of me so well and I have come to depend on you so much. I don't know what I'd do without you.

To my street team, AJ's Angels, I love every one of you with all my heart. You are so supportive and kind and are always willing to do anything to support me and my books. To Sandie, Bets, Jen, Suzanne, Andrea and all the other wonderful ladies I say a heartfelt Thank You!

To Anne, my proofreader, the readers say thank you. ;) As I furiously type away I am confident in knowing that you will take care of all my silly mistakes.

To my attorney, the amazing Sarah, also my daughter, I appreciate you always taking my calls. My children are my greatest achievement in life and no book will ever take that title.

To my marketing strategist Brad, you are brilliant and I am so happy I get to spend my life with you. Being your wife makes my heart content.

And to my son, Christopher, who wears so many hats there isn't enough space to list them all, I want you to know I wouldn't want to work with anyone else but you. Talent oozes from your pores - you are brilliant! I love you to the moon and back.

And finally, to all the readers who buy my books I say thank you. And to those of you who email me and

Facebook with me and send me the kindest messages, you will never know how much you mean to me and how you always lift my spirits and make my days brighter.

I have the best job in the world and I am sincerely grateful for all of you who continue to support me.

Table of Contents

1.	1
2.	17
3.	27
4.	39
5.	45
6.	55
7.	65
8.	71
9.	83
10.	91
11.	105
12.	119
13.	125
14.	133
15.	143
16.	151
17.	157
18.	165
19.	171
20.	179
21.	187
22.	195
23.	201
24.	209
25.	215
26.	229
27.	243
EPILOGUE	247
About AJ Harmon	250

1.

"Well? How do I look?" The sky blue satin clung to her firm, round breasts and cinched tight at the waist, flaring slightly as the delicate fabric fell to her feet, which were adorned with silver strappy stilettos. "It's new," Claire added as she twirled around in front of the mirror feeling like a princess. No response came, verbal or otherwise. "When I saw it in the dress shop window I thought it would be perfect for tonight. It fits like it was made especially for me." She continued to babble until he held up his hand.

"I prefer you in another color."

Claire tried to hide the disappointment that instantly washed over her. She'd spent all afternoon making sure her hair was perfectly coifed and her makeup was immaculate, desperately hoping that he'd approve of the way she looked. The dress was just supposed to be the icing on the cake.

"You should wear the black halter dress."

"I wore that to the opera last month," she replied. "But, I suppose I could…"

"Then the red strapless chiffon."

"Um, I don't think I have enough time to change," she said, biting her bottom lip, attempting to stop it from trembling. She wouldn't cry. He didn't like it when she cried.

"You do." His response was clipped and Claire understood that she was to change… now.

Standing in the bathroom just a moment later, she leaned on the granite counter for support and considered her tear-filled eyes in the mirror staring back at her. She'd used blue and silver eye shadow, to go with her new dress. Now she would be dressed in red and Claire knew he'd make a snide comment about her make-up not matching. There was no time to dwell on it now though. She had to change into the red chiffon… and quickly.

Pulling the gown from the plastic dry-cleaning bag, she unzipped the side zipper and laid it over the arm chair in her sprawling walk-in closet. Making quick work of the buckles on her Manolo Blahnik shoes, she kicked them off and then wriggled out of her dazzling princess dress, tossing it on the plush carpeted floor in a fit of anger. Why had she thought she could buy something without his approval? It was stupid of her to think he would like it. Experience had told her she'd been making a mistake. She squeezed herself into the requested attire, frustrated at the knowledge she'd be sitting for so long. It was a dress for standing due to the intricate beadwork on the bodice that cut into her flesh just below the bust when she sat for prolonged periods of time, and tonight would be one of those nights. Her posture would have to be perfect for the next four hours.

Slipping her feet into nude Prada pumps, Claire hurried back to the bathroom and grabbed a grey eye shadow and tried to lessen the blue of her eyelids by dabbing the powder-filled brush into the creases of her lids. Managing to soften the look and even succeed in bringing out the brilliant green of her eyes, she was satisfied with her effort.

"Claire!"

Her time was up. "Ready. Coming." With one more glance in the mirror she desperately hoped he would be happy with her appearance this time. As she stepped out of the bathroom she attempted a smile. "Better?"

With a grunt, he stood and walked to the door of their

bedroom. "We're late," he growled. "Come on."

Hiding her disappointment had become second nature. She could do it without even thinking. "Yes," she nodded. "I'm sorry." Grabbing her silver clutch on the way out, she wondered if he'd say something about the color of her accessories being poorly chosen. It was silly to wonder – of course he would!

*****

In the ladies room, Claire dabbed at her face with a tissue, making sure there was not a smudge to be seen on her perfectly painted face. Finally satisfied with her appearance she stepped into the hallway and stopped in her tracks. They stood several feet away and had no clue she was watching. He grabbed Greta's throat and shoved her against the wall.

"You will act like my loving wife or I will remind you again who's in charge," Philip threatened through gritted teeth.

Greta nodded as he released her and her hands went to her throat, rubbing the pain away. He turned abruptly and stomped away, in the opposite direction of Claire as she just stood there… rooted to the ground, watching as Greta burst into tears. Claire started towards her but a group of people entered the hallway from the other end and Greta lowered her head and disappeared in the crowd.

Several minutes later, back in the grand foyer of the magnificent hotel, Claire saw Greta and hurried over to her, concerned for her safety.

"You look lovely, as always," Greta smiled as she placed air kisses on each of Claire's cheeks.

"Thank you," Claire replied. "Are you okay?" She studied her neck looking for signs of the exchange she'd just witnessed.

"Oh, just fine, darling," Greta smiled. "Are you having a good time?"

"I didn't realize there would be so many people here."

"Oh, yes. Philip said on the way here that the entire executive management team were expected to be here. That's a lot of people."

"Yes, it is," Claire agreed.

Philip Westover owned Westover Manufacturing and had built it from nothing almost twenty years ago. It was now a Fortune 500 company and employed hundreds of thousands of people all over the globe. Claire had heard Philip's story many times; how he'd built his first company only to lose it due to a massive recall in the early eighties. He'd licked his wounds and bounced back, this time better and stronger, bigger and more powerful than before… blah blah blah. Yeah, she'd heard it a million times.

Greta was Philip's third wife, a little older than Claire, probably in her early thirties. She was like a thoroughbred, the daughter of one of Greece's elite, a shipping magnate. Raised in New York, Greta was educated at only the finest private schools. She and Philip had no children, but he had two grown daughters from his previous marriages. Claire wondered when the joyous news would be announced. After all, the only way for her to ensure a continued share of the wealth would be for Greta to have his baby. Being wife number three certainly would not instill any confidence in the marriage lasting and who wouldn't want a part of his empire?

"You and Brent are at our table, *obviously*," Greta smiled that fake shallow smile that Claire had come to recognize so well. "The riffraff will be kept away," she added.

"Riffraff?" Claire asked.

"Middle management," Greta whispered in hushed tones.

"Ah," she nodded. "The dreaded middle management," she mocked to an oblivious Greta.

"Ex-act-ly!"

She felt his hand on the small of her back. "You are the most beautiful woman in the room," he whispered in her ear.

"Thank you," Claire smiled, thrilled to hear that he was happy with her appearance.

He kissed her softly on the cheek and she instinctively leaned her face into his lips, desperate for the affection.

"Careful," Brent said as he straightened, pulling away. "You don't want to smudge your makeup."

"No," she frowned, the exhilaration quickly squashed.

Brent held his hand out and Claire took it as he led her through the throng of people to the table in the ballroom, front and center. "Are you ready to be proud of me?" he asked as he pulled her chair out.

"I'm always proud of you," Claire responded.

"Well then, tonight you'll be extra proud," he grinned. "I'm getting the big award."

"The *big* one?" Claire was surprised.

"Yep. Philip just told me. The bonus that comes with it is amazing."

"A bonus?"

Brent nodded. "Do you know what kind of car I'll be buying with it?"

Claire shook her head.

"No, neither do I, but it can be *any* car I want! Even a Lamborghini!" he whispered.

"Wow! That big, huh?"

He just smiled and looked around at everyone taking their seats. Claire was seated, her back perfectly straight, and Brent settled in next to her. Several months ago he'd told her that once he got a raise they'd get married, that he'd be ready to take the next step. They'd been living together for over two years in his townhouse that he'd had completely renovated right before she moved in. In fact, if she remembered right, he'd promised they'd get married once he was more *financially set.*

"Maybe, if the bonus is that big," she began, "we could think about setting a date."

His head whipped around, a flash of anger registered on his handsome features, and as quickly as it had appeared, it was gone. "It's a bonus not a raise. We discussed this."

"Yes, but if it's enough for a Lamborghini, maybe it's enough that…"

"Let's not discuss money in public. It's inappropriate," he scolded.

Biting her lip, Claire nodded. "Yes," she replied.

Philip and Greta arrived at the table and Brent stood and shook his boss' hand. They were joined by Alan, the CFO, and his wife, and Garrett, the head of the legal department and his partner. Champagne was poured and the men discussed business, as they did at every company function, while the women discussed which designer that had supplied their dresses for the evening. Claire nodded at the appropriate moments and Brent reached for her hand under the table as he was discussing marketing ideas for the next tradeshow. Feeling relief that he wasn't upset with her, she laced her fingers with his and took a breath, ready to play the perfect part for the rest of the evening.

*****

"Look at her!" the girls teased.

Claire's head lowered and she glanced at the old shoes on her feet, worn and well-loved. So worn that the holes grew in size each day. Hearing the girls tease her day after day was starting to grow old, but the sharp sting was there with each cutting remark. Ten year old girls could be cruel and it would only get worse as they got older.

Living on the wrong side of the tracks with a father who used to work construction but had been on disability since a fall from some scaffolding had left him unable to work, and a mother who was a cashier at the local drugstore, did not impress the girls in Claire's 5th grade class. Money had always been tight, but since the accident, new shoes were not a priority. Rent, electricity and medical needs topped the list. Shoes were near the bottom. It was only when she was at school that Claire noticed she was not dressed like the other girls, that her backpack was not the newest style, and that her perfectly comfortable shoes were not up to snuff.

"Mom," she whined one day after a particularly hard day at school. "I need new shoes. And a new backpack. And some new clothes."

"Claire," her mother had sighed while slipping her feet into the well-worn white sneakers. "There's no money for frivolous things like that. I have three dollars in my purse and that has to buy milk and bread to last the rest of the week till I get paid."

"And then I can have new shoes?" Claire replied hopefully.

"No, you can't."

"I never get anything new!" she wailed as she stomped off to her bedroom and slammed the door shut as she threw her bag to the floor. "I hate being poor," she muttered to herself. "When I grow up I'm never going to be poor. I'm going to have a hundred

pairs of shoes!"

*****

Carefully hanging his suit back on the hanger, Brent placed it in his closet and walked into the bathroom just as Claire was rinsing the makeup from her face.

"You were the most beautiful woman in the room tonight," he smiled proudly. "Every man there was jealous of me and every woman wanted to be you."

"I doubt that," Claire said as she shook her head.

"Of course they did! Every man there was dreaming of fucking you and every woman there was envisioning fucking me," he grinned. "But no man will ever fuck you except me. Remember that," he scowled as he stared at her reflection in the mirror.

"I don't want any man except you," Claire smiled. "You're my guy."

"Yes. Yes I am." Brent threw his socks and white dress shirt into the basket and headed for the bedroom. "Will you be long?"

"No. I'll join you in just a moment."

Brent nodded and left her as she scrubbed her face and rinsed it with cool water. Then she slathered the silky moisturizer over her face and neck and rubbed lotion into her hands and feet. Dressed in a satin nightie, Claire joined Brent in the king-sized bed and immediately curled into his side. He clicked off the lamp and turned to her kissing her soundly on the lips. Within moments she could feel his shaft pulsing into her hip. Inwardly smiling, the anticipation of him making passionate love to her was thrilling. It had been some time since they'd made love like they used to. In recent weeks it had been more mechanical than amorous, more indifferent than erotic.

Her hand reached for him and encircled his engorged manhood.

"Not your hand," he grunted as he pushed her away, shoving her shoulders down. "Blow me," he demanded. "I just need a quick release. I have to be in the office early in the morning."

"But it's Sunday," she frowned. "Aren't we going to..."

"I have to work. I have to pay for the dress you didn't wear tonight. Just suck me, please."

With the lights off he didn't see the overwhelming disappointment in her eyes as she scooted down the bed and did as he wished. Within a couple of minutes he'd rolled over and was already falling asleep. Claire tiptoed into the bathroom and rinsed her mouth with mouthwash and then padded downstairs and poured herself a drink. Sinking into the corner of the leather sectional in the family room, she clicked on the television and found the shopping channel. A new pair of shoes, or two, would lift her spirits. It usually did.

*****

Brent Cooper was a man of great determination. He set goals and then achieved them, and then he set more goals. At the ripe old age of 32 he had sprinted up the corporate ladder, becoming the youngest VP of marketing in the history of the company. He'd never been one to shy away from hard work and long hours and owed his success to his work ethic. Not necessarily the smartest, he overcame that slight disadvantage with an iron will – a will that had put him where he was today. Every man wanted to be him and every woman wanted to be with him.

Meeting Claire had come at the wrong time. Brent hadn't yet achieved his career goals and he'd just managed to scrape together the down payment on his luxury townhouse. Luxury only because of its size and address. It needed hundreds of thousands of dollars of work put into it before he would ever dream of having anyone over. A girlfriend was not in his plan… yet.

A favorite college professor had called him up out of the blue and asked him to come and speak to his business class. Brent had jumped at the chance for several reasons. He was thrilled with the idea of seeing his old mentor once again, and any excuse he could find to be put squarely in the spotlight he eagerly welcomed. It also didn't look bad to his subordinates that he was lecturing at the prestigious university from which he'd graduated just a few years earlier. Brent constantly heard the grumblings from members of his department about his lack of experience and obvious connection with the boss. How else could he have gotten the job? He'd been only 30, after all.

She'd been sitting in the fourth row… the aisle seat. Big innocent eyes and plump lips that were always slightly parted, giving her the look of being constantly surprised. He couldn't take his eyes of her and found himself tripping over his tongue on more than one occasion. Silently admitting to himself that she was the most heavenly creature he'd ever laid eyes on, he asked his old professor for a favor after class had ended. Deciding on the spot that he needed an intern, the professor was going to get him the doe-eyed beauty from row number four.

He'd followed through and somehow Brent had managed to convince his supervisor that he did indeed need an intern.

From the time Brent had entered college he'd had a plan with a timeline. The day before he'd met Claire he was on track, everything in order and on schedule. The girlfriend wasn't supposed to come until much later. He wanted his apartment completely renovated and he needed the promotion first to pay for it. She'd come too early but Brent knew gold when he saw it, and Claire was pure gold.

It all started very innocently. She came to work for him a few hours a week, when she didn't have class or work. She'd switched her schedule at the restaurant to the late shift so she could fit it all in, usually only sleeping a few hours a night before her long day started all over again. For the first couple of weeks he had her doing grunt work - girl Friday stuff - assignments normally given to a temp who didn't have much skill. But she quickly proved to be a very bright asset and Brent recognized her talent. He also recognized her potential and was threatened. It was ludicrous to think that she would ever get his job, but being the insecure man that he was, his thoughts were not always rational.

"You know, we have a full-time spot for you. All you have to do is say the word and I'll make it happen," he told her one night after the building was dark and quiet. They'd stayed late to finish up a report the board had requested to have the next morning.

"Really?" she'd replied, those big expressive eyes registering shock and delight.

"Really," he smiled.

"It's so tempting," she sighed. "But I need to finish school. I have two semesters left and I would hate to not graduate now."

"You can always go back and finish," he scoffed. "Opportunities like this don't come around very often. It's literally being placed in your lap. I think you'd be crazy not to at least sleep on it."

With the hint of a smile, she agreed to sleep on it.

It worked. She started full time in the office the following month, once the school semester was over. Brent received an angry call from his old professor. He let it go to his voicemail. He listened to the first few seconds of being chastised for snatching Claire's future from her and then he deleted the message, his conscience clear. He'd given her an opportunity, at least, that's the way he chose to view his offer.

Within the next year, Brent received the promotion he was hoping for, and with it the funds necessary to begin the massive undertaking of renovating his home – a townhouse that had been converted to three apartments, now being converted back to one family home. He wanted a family one day, far into the future, and this real estate acquisition would be perfect. First, however, he had to woo Claire.

Everyone who met Claire loved her. She was a beauty, but she was also kind and considerate and had a great sense of humor. At first her new coworkers were skeptical, but she'd quickly proved her worth and was accepted as an asset to the company. She learned the ropes rapidly and was heading up projects that were being completed timely and with great praise.

One evening after most of the employees had gone home, Brent stuck his head into her cubicle and asked her if she'd like to join him for dinner. He saw the hesitation in her expression and calmed her nerves by saying it was just two coworkers grabbing a bite and then sharing a cab home, so she agreed.

There was a little Chinese restaurant on the next block and they walked in a light rain, laughing as they jumped over puddles. Dinner was pleasant and when it was time to leave and she reached for the bill, Brent laughed and said he'd put it on his company credit card. Walking outside, noting the rain had stopped, he hailed a cab, but Claire graciously declined, said thank you for the meal and walked swiftly around the corner, disappearing into the night. For a first step, Brent was pleased how well it had gone.

The following week he asked her to dinner again. She smiled and nodded, asking if there was a good pizza place nearby. She'd been dying for a slice all day.

"Your wish is my command," he grinned and bowed as she stood and slung her purse over her shoulder.

It only took a couple more spontaneous dinner dates when Brent was ready to launch his full attack. Wining and dining her was easy and it didn't take much to cast his spell and she'd fallen… hard. Several times a week they'd have lunch together and most evenings they went out for dinner after work, laughing and sharing stories from their past and falling in love more and more.

One evening, after a romantic dinner, Brent suggested they go back to her place.

"I've waited 'til I thought you were ready… for the right moment… and I think this is it. I want to feel you under me. I want to feel your skin against my lips. I want to peel the clothes from your body and explore every inch of you." His desire was genuine but he saw fear in her eyes as he spoke. "Don't be afraid," he whispered. "I just want to love you."

With a weak smile as she lowered her eyelids, Claire found the courage to tell him the secret she'd been hiding from him all these months. "I'm afraid that… that my home… my house won't be up to your standards. You're sophisticated and rich and I'm not either of those things. I'm afraid you won't want to be with me after you see where I come from."

"Nonsense," he soothed. "I'm in love with you, not the roof that you have over your head. You don't know me at all if you think I can be put off so easily."

Hand in hand they sat in the back of a cab as they drove to her home, a single wide trailer in a trailer park about twenty miles from the city. Holding her breath, Claire waited for Brent's reaction as she unlocked the door and walked inside. He said nothing, just pulled her into his arms and kissed her until he whispered, "Where's the bedroom?" and then they didn't speak at all 'til dawn.

*****

Within just a few short weeks, Claire would have done *anything* for Brent. She was consumed by him and convinced that he was the one who would make her life complete. He was the one with whom she wanted to have a bunch of children. And he was most definitely the one that she wanted in her bed every night. She was sure that he felt the same way. But then…

One night, on their way to her house, she asked, "Why don't you ever drive your car?"

"I'm not gonna have it stolen, or stripped," he frowned. "I'll leave it safely in the garage… that has security."

She didn't let him see her face. She'd been afraid that he'd be ashamed of her and her suspicions seemed to be correct. Yet when she broached the subject with him, he dismissed it, telling her she was imagining things and to let it go, so she tried.

And then it happened. Brent was promoted to VP, the position he'd been working for nonstop for the last nine years. They celebrated by flying to Las Vegas for the weekend. Claire was ecstatic. She'd never been west of the Mississippi River and had certainly never flown first class. They were treated as VIPs everywhere they went and she loved every second.

However, on Monday morning when she arrived back at work, she was called to the HR office, and the fairytale came to a crashing halt.

"But," she began, almost in tears. "I don't understand since he isn't my direct supervisor. It hasn't been a problem up until now," she stuttered as she held back the tears that were threatening to fall.

"It's different now that he is the VP of the department." She was being let go.

It seemed monumentally unfair that she couldn't even transfer to another department. They all required four year college degrees and she didn't have one. She'd left school to work with Brent and now that his dreams were coming true, hers were crashing around her feet. Brent didn't seem overly concerned when she burst into his office and threw herself into his arms sobbing hysterically.

"You don't have to work," he shrugged. "I'll take care of you. It's all fine."

And it was… for a little while.

2.

With breakfast consumed, Brent out the door promptly at 8:15 and the dirty dishes in the dishwasher, Claire wriggled into her workout clothes, grabbed her bag and headed for the gym. There was a gym a couple of blocks from the townhouse, but when she'd started work at Westover Manufacturing she'd splurged and bought a membership at the gym on the same block as the company headquarters. It was further away from where she lived but she felt comfortable there and didn't want to change. Within thirty minutes she was on the elliptical machine working up a sweat and feeling her muscles work in unison with each step. Weight training came next. Not to build muscle – just to maintain it. Brent had told her numerous times that women didn't look good fat and he had no intention of ever being married to anyone who didn't know how to maintain the body worthy of his affection. Claire had taken him seriously and visited the gym four times a week without fail and often threw in a long run if the weather was nice. There would not ever be a reason for Brent to find her unattractive. She would make sure of that.

One of the benefits of working out was being able to clear her mind for a couple of hours. Normally her thoughts flitted from this to that and on to something else. Concentrating on her workout allowed her brain to rest, if just for a little while. Sadly, once she was in the dressing room, showering and getting ready for the day, all those thoughts came roaring back.

From the outside it appeared that Claire had everything any woman could ever dream of. She no longer had a job that demanded her attention. Brent was the kind of man every woman wanted. He was gorgeous, rich, and knew how to spoil his woman. Their glamorous home was something out of a magazine and a cleaning service came in three days a week to make sure it was always looking its best. Her Chanel wallet contained her driver's license and one credit card – a black American Express. She was able to purchase anything she wanted, any time she wanted. Being a regular at several exclusive boutiques in the city enabled her to always have the newest fashion… and the most expensive. A standing appointment every six weeks at a swanky salon kept her hair the perfect blend of blonde and honey with a hint of copper that caught the sunlight giving a brilliant effect of light and dark. Groceries were delivered and put away regularly and four nights a week a private chef came in to prepare their evening meal. Yes, from the outside her life looked perfect, indeed.

With her red leather pencil skirt zipped, her white silk long-sleeved blouse buttoned and tucked in, her black Christian Louboutin ankle boots on and black Chanel purse draped elegantly over her arm, Claire walked into the late morning sun and headed in the direction of Brent's office. It was a risk surprising him. Driven by a need for control, surprises weren't one of his favorite things. He liked order and Claire hoped he wouldn't mind her dropping by unannounced.

His secretary smiled as she entered his office and she lifted the telephone and announced his visitor and nodded for Claire to go in. Brent stood as she opened the door and rounded the large wooden desk and kissed her cheek.

"To what do I owe this unexpected visit?"

"I just left the gym and wondered if you were available for lunch?" Claire asked hopefully.

Brent frowned with genuine regret. "I wish I could but I'm booked solid for the rest of the day."

"Oh well," Claire shrugged. "Maybe another time?"

"Yes. Definitely. Another time. I'll see you at home this evening."

With another peck on her cheek, Brent went back to his chair and back to work leaving Claire to see herself out. As she passed the executive offices on the way to the elevator, she made a quick stop in the ladies room.

"Oh, Greta!" she exclaimed. "Hello!" She was happy to see a friendly face but as Greta turned her face to her, Claire couldn't hide the horror from her expression. "What happened?"

"It's my fault," Greta muttered as she turned back to the mirror, dabbing concealer on her cheek to hide the ugly purple bruise. "I know better than to argue with him when he's stressed."

"What? Philip did this to you?" She was truly horrified.

With a slight shrug of her shoulder Greta smirked at her reflection. "It's not the first time and I seriously doubt it will be the last, even though he promises me it will be. He'll come home with a fabulous piece of jewelry tonight and it will all be forgotten."

Her dismissal of the situation horrified Claire even more. "Surely you can't go on living like that?"

"You don't understand," Greta snapped. "I am not leaving this marriage. Besides, it's more common than you think."

"That doesn't mean it's okay."

"Claire," Greta smiled. "I will be just fine. And I don't want you telling anyone about this. It's just our little secret, okay?"

With a nod, Claire agreed to not say a word.

"Are you free for lunch and some shopping this afternoon?" Greta asked.

"Actually, I am."

"Great! Let's go do some damage," she grinned.

*****

Weeks passed and life went on as usual. Brent went to work, they socialized with the elite on the weekends and even managed to get away a couple of times. There were moments when Claire felt the magic back… Brent was loving and sensitive, attentive and generous. Sex was making love once more with Brent giving as he'd done in the beginning. Claire felt cherished and wanted and the closeness they felt was everything she'd hoped to recapture. The future for them was bright and Claire felt content and happy.

But there was Greta. Claire saw her several times and each encounter had her worrying more as she noted a slight change in her friend's behavior. Greta was less outgoing and her fashion choices were no longer daring and sexy. Sweaters and button-up blouses became the norm and Claire wondered if she was hiding bruises. With Greta wearing sunglasses during lunch one afternoon, Claire reached for her friend's hand across the table and squeezed in a show of support.

"Greta," she began. "This can't go on anymore."

"What?" Greta chided. "You don't know what you're talking about. Everything is just fine. There are times when I forget to be quiet. I can be quite demanding. It isn't his fault."

"But…"

"Please, Claire. We won't discuss it. Let's just enjoy our lunch."

It was the dismissal that worried Claire just as much as the hidden bruises. That evening as she and Brent were sharing a glass of Brandy after dinner she broached the subject with him.

"Does Philip ever talk about his wife?"

"Huh?"

"Have you ever heard Philip talk about Greta when she isn't around?"

Brent looked at her with a furrowed brow.

"He hits her," she continued.

A response didn't come. In fact, it appeared her words were not understood at all.

"She's bruised all over and says it's her fault that he beats her."

"Maybe it is," he shrugged.

"What? You can't be serious?"

"Don't be naïve. A woman can drive a man mad. It certainly isn't his fault if she angers him enough that he needs to correct her. Greta probably brings it on herself."

Claire decided to drop the subject. She was stunned with his response. How could he think it was okay to hit a woman? She was just relieved that he wasn't the abusive type. But it didn't stop her from worrying about her friend.

"Come to bed," Brent whispered. He held out his hand and she laced her fingers with his. "Don't think about anybody else but me," he grinned.

"I can do that," she smiled as she followed him up the stairs.

*****

"Oh, I'm so sorry," Claire exclaimed as she rounded the corner in the locker room at the gym. "I wasn't looking where I was going."

"Me either," the woman laughed. "I love your shoes!"

"Thanks," smiled Claire. "They are really comfortable and who doesn't love pink?"

"I love pink. I'm Rebekah."

"Claire."

The two women smiled at each other and bonded over tennis shoes and sports bras for several minutes making an instant friendship.

"I've seen you here many times," Rebekah said.

"I've been coming here for a few years."

"Me too. I work close by so it's pretty convenient. I take an early lunch and spend it here most days. But I have to admit I would much prefer to be having lunch. I love food too much which is why I spend an hour a day here," she laughed.

"Oh how I love food," Claire sighed. "But I rarely get to eat what I love," she frowned. "Those damn size two dresses in my closet mock me every time I look at a piece of cheesecake."

"We are a slave to fashion and to the designers who tell us what we look good in," Rebekah winked. "Maybe though, we can cheat every now and then and have lunch?"

"I'd love that," Claire beamed.

They exchanged phone numbers, said their goodbyes and went their separate ways.

Since Claire had left Westover Manufacturing, her circle of friends had shrunk considerably. There were not many opportunities for her to meet new people and so meeting Rebekah had been delightful and Claire waited all of three hours before texting her and making a lunch date for the following week. A reply came back immediately and the time and place were chosen. With a spring in her step, Claire left the gym, walked confidently to her black BMW and drove home.

The cleaning service took care of the house, but Claire did the laundry. There was something creepy about having strangers washing her panties. She preferred to take care of it herself, and she enjoyed ironing Brent's dress shirts. In a small way she felt it showed him how much she loved him. After she'd emptied her gym bag, she began sorting colors to get the clothes cleaned and put away.

With a smile and a shake of her head, Claire emptied the pockets of Brent's jeans before stuffing them in the washer and then checked his suit pockets before she made a pile to go to the dry cleaners. Gum wrappers, handkerchiefs, even a couple of business cards ended up on the counter before she was done. And then…

A napkin. A phone number. A name. Lisa. The i dotted with a heart. *No!*

*****

"I'll be a little late."

"Oh?" She couldn't hide the disappointment in her voice.

"It's just a meeting that shouldn't go too long," Brent added. "I should be home by nine or so. How about a late dinner? We could go to Arnie's?"

"Yes," Claire whispered. "That would be nice." *He's going to be late. Is it Lisa?*

"Okay. I'll see you later." He hung up leaving Claire

staring at her cell phone wondering if he really had a meeting.

A little before seven o'clock she called his office, hoping he'd answer. He didn't. In all likelihood there was a perfectly reasonable explanation for the napkin in his pocket. She'd never had a reason to distrust him before. Yet, the nagging in the back of her mind pecked away at her until she was in a state of complete anxiety. Somehow she had to pull herself together before he got home and they went to dinner.

With a great deal of energy and discipline, Claire dressed and primped and was as gorgeous as ever at 8:55pm when Brent walked in the front door. He dumped his briefcase on the chair by the door and walked straight to the crystal jug that held his brandy and poured a drink.

"I swear I am the only person that knows anything at these fucking meetings," he snarled. "These old geezers that watch Mad Men and think that's how business works today are just fucking idiots."

"I'm sorry," Claire soothed as she rubbed his shoulders. "Would you prefer to stay in?"

"No," he shook his head. "You look damn hot. I think I'll show you off tonight." He emptied his drink in one mouthful, slammed the glass down on the table and grabbed her hand. "Let's go eat and then we'll come back here and I'll fuck your brains out."

Claire decided it was not the right time to bring up the napkin and the mystery woman named Lisa. They had a scrumptious meal at Arnie's and came back and, as promised, Brent fucked her brains out. He'd never been quite that rough before, grabbing at her hair and leaving bruises as he slammed into her over and over again. Stress at work had triggered this kind of behavior from him before but it seemed as though each incident he got rougher and rougher. It wasn't satisfying for her at all, but it appeared to be what he needed so she went along with it until he was exhausted and fell into a sound sleep.

Creeping quietly to the bathroom, Claire drew herself a hot bath and sunk into the scalding water. Just a few days ago her life was near perfect. Brent still hadn't proposed but she was sure it was close. But now? Now she felt sure about nothing. Sinking under the water, she closed her eyes and felt the sting of the water on her bruised skin, the fingernail scratches down her thighs and back. She'd known passion with Brent but this had been something very different. In an unsettling way she knew there'd been a shift. But she couldn't put her finger on it. Lying in the tub until the water grew cool, Claire wondered what was to come.

3.

People come into your life for a reason and Claire knew immediately that Rebekah would be a friend for life. They were the same age, although Rebekah was married and had a three year old daughter. They had the same taste in books, in music, in movies, and in food. Without any discussion beforehand they ordered the same items on the menu for lunch, right down to the raspberry vinaigrette on their green salad. There wasn't a quiet moment during the fifty minute lunch date. They were both sorry to see it come to an end and made a date for the following week - same place, same time.

The next seven days couldn't go fast enough for Claire. She was surprised at how eager she was to meet Rebekah. It had been a long time since she had a friend that was her very own. All her friends were in one way or another connected to Brent, but Rebekah wasn't. She was hers, all hers. When Thursday morning arrived, Claire was almost giddy with anticipation.

"What's wrong with you?" Brent asked as she danced around the kitchen making his coffee and toast.

"Nothing."

"Are you high?"

That made her laugh. "Don't be silly. Of course not. I'm just happy."

"About what?"

"About life."

"Whatever," he muttered as he chewed his toast and sipped his coffee.

She kissed him on the cheek as he lifted his briefcase

from the chair by the front door and danced up the stairs to get ready for her lunch date. With Florence & the Machine blaring from her stereo, Claire showered and dressed smartly in tan dress slacks, a crisp white linen shirt and black pumps and her Gucci purse. She slipped silver earrings through her ears and a chunky silver cuff on her wrist. A couple of squirts of her favorite Dolce & Gabbana perfume and she was ready to go.

It seemed as if the traffic lights had some kind of beef with her as she hit every red light in the city, but eventually made it to the restaurant and even found a parking spot just a block away. Rebekah spotted her hurrying up the sidewalk and the two women hugged like long lost friends and hooked arms as they entered the restaurant and were seated immediately. In what felt like only a few minutes, their hour had come to an end. Both women were frustrated that it was time for them to leave.

"You should come to our book club," Rebekah suggested. "We meet once a month, the first Friday of the month. Tomorrow. Can you come?"

"Ah, well I can try."

Rebekah gave her the address of her home and the novel they were reading. "But we don't really care about the book," she grinned. "It's really just an excuse to get together and drink wine and eat chocolate."

"Well, that sounds wonderful," Claire grinned. "Let me see what I can do." And with a hug, they said their goodbyes and Rebekah hurried back to the law firm she worked at as a paralegal and Claire strolled back to her car wondering how Brent would feel about her going to a book club. Would it be better to be honest with him, or should she just make up a reasonable excuse that he would believe.

"Why should I have to lie?" she asked herself as she

unlocked her car and slid inside. "It's a book club! How could he be upset with that?" And with that she drove home, stopping at Barnes and Noble on the way to buy the book that would be the discussion the following evening.

*****

With a bottle of Dominio del Plata Nosotros, Claire knocked on the door of the modest house in the quaint little subdivision. Most of the houses looked the same, were on small lots, but they were well-kept and she couldn't help but smile as she noted the number of basketball hoops adorning the garages and bikes and other kid paraphernalia scattered over green manicured lawns. Rebekah swung open the door and pulled Claire into a warm embrace.

"I'm so glad you could make it. Come in. Let me introduce you to the other girls."

Claire followed her in after giving Rebekah the wine and was warmly welcomed by the other three women sitting around the island in the kitchen. Scattered before them were some skillfully decorated chocolate cupcakes, a box of Russell Stover's, chocolate covered strawberries and some brownies dusted heavily with powdered sugar.

"Can you get diabetes from looking at food?" Claire joked.

"This is our once a month binge," Rachel grinned. She was Rebekah's sister, but Claire immediately knew they were from the same family. The dark hair and big brown eyes were a giveaway. The other two women were from the neighborhood.

"You all live around here?" Claire asked.

"Within three blocks of each other," Rachel replied. "My parents live just on the other side of the freeway, just a few minutes from here and our brother lives just down the street from them."

"It's nice to be close," Rebekah chimed in. "Built in babysitters are never more than ten minutes away," she chuckled. "Let's open this bottle and start the drinking."

"Um," Teresa interrupted. "That bottle of wine must have cost a bundle."

All eyes swung to Claire. "I just grabbed it from the wine cellar," she gulped.

"You have a wine cellar?" sang the women almost in unison.

"Well, Brent does," Claire admitted with embarrassment.

"Is that your husband?"

With a shake of her head she replied, "No. We aren't married."

"Maybe we shouldn't open it and you can take it home," Rebekah fretted.

"Nonsense!" Claire smiled. "It's for us tonight. I'll pour." And with that the wine was opened and poured into 5 plastic cups. She couldn't help but snicker when she thought of what Brent would do if he knew she was drinking a bottle of $130 wine in cheap plastic cups.

*****

It had been one of the most enjoyable nights she'd ever had. Claire felt relaxed and comfortable with her new friends. They'd drank, gorged themselves on chocolate, discussed the book of the month for a short while and laughed like she'd never laughed before. Tears cascaded down her perfectly rouged cheeks as she'd gasped for breath and ended up collapsed on the floor in the fetal position with Rebekah over practically nothing. But by that time of the evening, everything was hysterically funny. They weren't drunk - not even close – but bonded in friendship, the likes she'd never experienced before.

As Claire drove home the smile was still plastered on her face. In fact, her cheeks ached from smiling so much. It was a good ache.

"So much for a quick drink with a friend," Brent scowled as she walked into the kitchen.

"Sorry," Claire sobered.

"You said you'd be home about eight. It's after eleven."

"Oh, wow!" Claire exclaimed, shocked it was so late. "I had no idea I'd been out so long."

"I've been waiting. Did you even consider that I was here waiting?" His tone had an edge and Claire couldn't help but see the anger in his eyes.

"I'm very sorry," she repeated.

"And that's supposed to make it all better? I could have gone out tonight with one of my friends. I could have been having a great time too, but I chose to be here with you. Too bad you don't feel the same."

"Brent, come on. I rarely go out. In fact, I can't remember the last time I did. I'm sorry I'm late. Really. Let's just go to bed, okay?"

"So that you can fuck me and make me forgive you?" His voice was harsh and his eyes cold. Claire couldn't understand what had come over him.

"I don't think there is anything to forgive. I went out with a friend and now I'm home. Can we just move past it?"

"You ungrateful bitch!" he spat.

Now she was really dumbfounded. She'd never seen this ugly side of him and it scared her. Greta's face came to her mind. Claire backed away and positioned herself on the other side of the island. Brent took a step towards her.

"It was very inconsiderate of me," she whispered. "I should have come home much earlier, perhaps set an alarm so that the time didn't get away from me. I promise Brent, it will *never* happen again."

With a deep breath he stood in place and stared at her. Eventually the harshness of his expression softened and the Brent she loved slowly returned. "Let's just go to bed then," he conceded.

As Claire rinsed cool water over her face, the trembling continued. What had come over him? How could he have reacted so out of character? She was baffled with the whole thing. Maybe book club at Rebekah's was not such a great idea. She certainly didn't want to aggravate Brent. Claire brushed her hair, slipped a silk nightgown over her head and padded softly through to the bedroom. He was already asleep. A wave of relief washed over her as she climbed into bed, rolled onto her side and tried to sleep.

The next morning all had been forgotten, or so it seemed. Brent was back to his usual cheerful self and suggested they spend the day looking for antiques for the house to which she excitedly agreed.

They held hands, joked over lunch at a small out of the way diner and bought a couple of pieces that were perfect for the hallway on the second floor. By the time they arrived home just before dinner, everything really was all forgotten and her Brent was back to stay.

All was picture-perfect for the next few days. They held hands and ate popcorn while snuggling on the sofa and watched a movie. They made love in the shower and Brent came home from work on Tuesday with a magnificent gold bangle with the words *Mine Forever* inscribed on the inside. It was exquisite and as he placed it on her arm he held her wrist and kissed it, looking into her eyes and telling her she was, in fact, his. Claire smiled and threw her arms around his neck.

"I am," she smiled as she kissed him. "Forever."

*****

Thursday morning arrived and as usual, Claire sent Brent off to work with a full tummy and a kiss on the cheek. Then it was time to get ready for her lunch date with Rebekah. As anxious as she was to meet her friend, she also felt a slight apprehension. She would have to tell Rebekah that she couldn't come to book club next month, even though she desperately wanted to join her new friends for another gut-busting fun-filled night.

Pulling up to the restaurant Claire waved at Rebekah already standing on the sidewalk. Quickly slipping into an empty parking space, Claire grabbed her purse and hurried up the street to where Rebekah was waiting with a warm hug. Their instant closeness made it that much harder to pull back.

Why should Brent be able to dictate who I see and when? she asked herself. *Why does he get to decide how I spend every minute of my day?* And with that thought she said nothing about not being able to attend book club anymore and had every intention of buying the new book on her way home. She could read what she wanted and socialize when she chose. Brent wasn't going to dictate that. He didn't own her.

*****

Although they slept in the same bed, Claire didn't see much of Brent over the next couple of weeks. A new product coming to market meant the marketing department was in overdrive. He went to the office early, came home late, and worked most of the weekend. Even though Claire missed him, she was just the tiniest bit relieved that the subject of her going to Rebekah's again never came up. She went about her days as usual. Until...

Checking his pockets was routine. Once, and only once, had she not and ended up sending a very important business card to the cleaners, never to be seen again. Brent was livid with her, even though she wanted to point out that he was a grown man who should be able to empty his pockets before changing. She kept that thought to herself. Lesson learned, however. From that moment on, she *always* checked his pockets.

Lisa's phone number on the napkin was still fresh on her mind when she pulled a matchbook from his jacket's breast pocket. It was an expensive hotel and for the briefest of moments Claire allowed her mind to run. It was probably just a meeting with an ad agency or someone from work she told herself. But when his steel blue dress shirt had a smudge of what looked like lipstick on it, she couldn't stop the barrage of images from flashing through her mind. Was it possible? Is this Lisa woman a threat to her and her relationship with the man she loved? Would she ever be enough for a man?

*****

From the moment she'd set eyes on him she couldn't think of anything, or anyone else. Claire was a junior at Franklin High School and chemistry had been her least favorite class. Having to take a science class she'd chosen chemistry over biology after hearing the horror stories of having to dissect a frog. Mr. Hatton was a boring teacher and Claire had suffered through the first term and managed to eke out a B. But when Lance transferred in at the beginning of the second term Claire suddenly enjoyed the class.

A senior, a wide receiver on the football team and a forward on the basketball team, big blue eyes and dimples, Lance was every girls' dream, and he sat next to her! Granted, it was the only empty seat, but still. He was sitting next to her every day.

Claire was naturally shy – an introvert. Lance was outgoing and personable and it didn't take him long to coax her out of her shell. When he told her that chemistry was his favorite class of the day she blushed something fierce and he'd just grinned.

When the term ended, they both had received A's and Lance told her he'd never gotten an A before. She was obviously his good luck charm. So on the first day of the third, and final, term of the school year, he made sure to sit next to her again. Claire tried to hide her excitement. He was the first boy to ever pay her any attention and she fell head first into a massive crush. When he asked her for a study date the weekend before a big exam, she could hardly voice her affirmative reply. They went to the local library and then had pizza after at his family's restaurant. It had been the perfect evening, even though not technically a date. When he dropped her off at home he leaned over the console in his truck and kissed her on the cheek, expressed his sincere thanks for her help and she climbed from the car and floated to the front door of her house. Once in her room, she stared at her reflection in the mirror and the spot on her cheek that had touched his warm lips and she knew she was in love.

There is something sublimely magical about a first love. The endless possibilities manifested themselves in her dreams and by the time Monday morning came, she was so head over heels gone she could barely speak to him. He just smiled.

Over the next couple of weeks, preparations for prom were in full swing. The idea that he just might ask her sent Claire into another tailspin. The subject had come up a couple of times and he'd almost hinted that there was a possibility he might ask her.

"I don't have a date yet. Do you?" he'd asked.

Claire just shook her head and lowered her eyelids, unable to look at him.

"Maybe we can fix that," he'd grinned.

As much as she desperately wanted to go with him, the thought that pushed itself to the forefront of her mind was being able to find a dress when she had no money. Her parents' financial situation had not improved. In fact, it had worsened. Claire's father had needed back surgery again and money was even tighter. How on earth she could manage to find a dress and shoes for prom was beyond her so she tried not to think about it.

The Friday before prom, at the end of chemistry class, Lance asked Claire to have lunch with him. She quickly agreed. They sat outside on the retaining wall at the front of the school. They pulled their lunch from their brown paper sacks and nibbled on their sandwiches.

"You know, prom is next week," he began.

"It is."

"Hey Lance!" It was Anna, the head cheerleader and most popular girl in school. She stood in front of them dressed in the latest fashion, her make-up perfectly applied and her hair in golden curls that surrounded her heart-shaped face and pouty lips. "My dad has rented a limo for prom. A bunch of us are going and I need *you to go with me.* Please*?"*

Claire's heart plummeted as she watched Lance smile and jump off the wall. "Of course I'll go in your limo," he replied. "Text me all the details."

"You are my knight in shining armor," Anna beamed as she turned and skipped away.

As Lance turned away and looked at Claire's face, he knew what he'd done. Her expression said it all.

"I'm sorry," he sputtered. "I…"

"Oh, don't worry about it," she shrugged, struggling to cover her devastating disappointment. "You're gonna have a great time. I gotta go. See ya Monday." She jumped off the wall and all but ran into the school and straight to the bathroom where she hid for as long as possible before having to go to her next class.

*****

Claire stood in Brent's closet holding the matchbook in

her fingers. The memories of high school flooding her thoughts. She wasn't enough for Lance. He'd made that clear when he'd chosen Anna over her for prom. Now, living with the man of her dreams, had he chosen someone else too? Would she ever satisfy a man completely?

4.

With the wooden hanger in his hands, Brent folded his suit trousers and hung them on the hanger and then carefully placed his jacket on the hanger and placed it on the rod amongst his other expensive Italian suits. His pale blue dress shirt was discarded into the hamper, followed by his socks. He removed his Cartier watch and placed it in the top drawer. His eyes stopped as he saw the napkin and matchbook placed at the edge of the dresser.

"Is this supposed to mean something," he seethed as he stomped into the bedroom.

Sound asleep, Claire didn't stir until he screamed her name.

"If you want to know about this," he growled, the napkin and matchbook scrunched in his fist, "Then fucking ask. I'm swamped at work and I don't need your passive aggressive bullshit when I get home."

"Huh?" she asked, slowly sitting up and wiping the sleep from her eyes.

"You want to know who Lisa is?" Brent asked as he tossed the napkin at her. "She's probably some whore who wanted to blow me. I said no, although God knows why. At least she wouldn't be emotionally draining."

"Brent," Claire whispered, biting her bottom lip, steadying her chin from trembling. "I just left them there because I found them in your pockets. I know you don't want me throwing anything away."

"I didn't sleep with her," he repeated. "I didn't even know she'd stuck that in my pocket. As for the matchbook," he said as he turned it over and over in his fingers. "We met with the ad agency that's pitching some commercial ideas. It was nothing more than that. I don't even remember picking it up," he said, more to the matchbook than to her.

"I meant nothing," she choked. "I didn't mean to make you angry."

Brent stared at her, his features hard. Claire couldn't stop it as a single tear fell down her cheek. She quickly wiped it away and looked back at Brent.

"I'm sorry," he said as his shoulders slumped and he sat down on the end of the bed. "Work is so stressful. I feel as though I'm just going to snap."

Claire jumped from under the covers and knelt behind him, her fingers working the muscles in his tense shoulders. "It's okay," she soothed. "I didn't think anything of them," she said as she glanced at the crumpled napkin on the bed beside her. "I thought that if you didn't need it anymore that you'd throw it away."

"You are a good girl," Brent sighed. "Please forgive me."

"There's nothing to forgive," Claire smiled. "Come to bed and get some sleep. It's late."

He nodded and climbed under the comforter next to her and she cradled him in her arms.

"Just sleep," she whispered into his hair.

Within moments she could hear his deep breathing and knew he was asleep. She continued to stroke his hair as she tried to calm her nerves. She'd not seen him that angry. Telling herself it was just the stress at work, Claire closed her eyes and matched his breathing as she fell back asleep.

The next morning when she awoke, Brent was already gone from the house. It was only seven so he must have gone early. After wrapping herself in her robe, she wandered downstairs and found a note on the island in the kitchen.

Sorry. Dinner tonight?

A faint smile crossed her lips. She grabbed her phone from her purse, quickly typing in a text to him.

Dinner would be wonderful. Name the place and time and I'll meet you there. Love you.

That evening she was met with an enormous bouquet of flowers and a blue velvet box.

"What's this?" she asked in surprise.

"Open it," he smiled.

Inside was a stunning tennis bracelet.

"Do you like it?" he asked.

"It's beautiful," Claire gushed.

"Let me help you." Brent carefully removed it from the box and wrapped it around her wrist, clasping the ends together. "It looks stunning on you. I knew it would."

"You didn't have to."

"I did." Brent lowered his eyes and looked ashamed. "I was cruel last night. I was an ass and I should never have spoken to you like that. I'm sorry."

"It's all forgotten," Claire smiled and placed her hand on his cheek. "I love you."

"I love you too."

The evening was all that Claire could have imagined. Brent was warm and happy and they made love when they returned home. Life was all as it should be.

*****

Going to the opera was not an unusual event for Claire. They went at least once or twice a year. This year they'd been invited to join Philip and Greta in their box. Carmen was being performed and Claire had never seen it before. She was looking forward to it and looking forward to dressing up in her finest and having a lovely time.

However the night before was book club at Rebekah's. Claire had read the book and was ready to discuss it in depth, even though she knew they'd probably just drink a large amount of wine and laugh all evening. She smiled as she got herself ready.

Brent was working late… again. He'd said they were close to being finished with the roll-out campaign so life would get back to normal in a few weeks. Claire longed for being normal again. It had been too tense for far too long. She was ready… *longing* for normal.

Driving to Rebekah's house Claire couldn't hide her smile. They'd had a fabulous lunch the day before at a brand new sushi place and she was excited to have some friends outside of Westover Manufacturing and she really, really liked these women. She arrived at Rebekah's and was once again warmly welcomed and she wasn't disappointed - she had a fabulous time. They drank some wine, ate some chocolate and laughed so much she even slightly wet her pants. She was mortified until Rachel admitted having done the same thing, and then they laughed more. Just like Cinderella, the clock struck midnight and Claire knew she had to go. She'd already stayed way longer than she'd planned and she just hoped that Brent wasn't home yet.

They picked their book for the next month and said their goodbyes. Claire hurried to her car and climbed inside. She put the key in the ignition and turned, but nothing happened. Her car wouldn't start.

"Oh, shit!"

*****

Brent sat in an armchair in the family room, a crystal tumbler in his hand. He'd downed his fourth drink waiting for Claire to return. He had no idea where she was or who she was with. He was getting angrier by the second.

He'd handpicked Claire. He could have had any woman he wanted and he wanted Claire. She should be forever grateful that he'd chosen her despite her less than perfect background. Men like him didn't pick girls from the wrong side of the tracks, yet he had. He'd plucked her from a trailer park in a less than desirable suburb and placed her in the most exclusive part of the city in a multimillion dollar townhouse. She had a massive walk-in closet and a credit card to fill up that closet with the finest fashion money could buy. Her jewelry box was filled with precious gems and she only ever wore an expensive handbag on her arm, one with a name that other women would envy. Yes, she should be eternally grateful.

Yet here he sat on a Friday night, well after midnight, not knowing where she was. He'd been given no indication she was going out. *Selfish bitch!*

5.

Ezekiel Dayton was sitting on his bed in his comfortable home with a beer in his hand and the television remote in his other hand when his cell phone rang. In his line of work, his work phone rang all hours of the day and night, but this was his personal cell.

“Hello?”

“Hey Zeke.”

Rebekah. “Hey, sis. You’re up late.”

“Can you come and help my friend? Her car won’t start.”

“Where are you?” he asked.

“In my driveway.”

“I’ll be right over.” He put the beer down, fortunately the first one of the night, grabbed his keys, slung his well-worn leather jacket over his broad shoulders and walked outside. He wanted to ride his motorcycle seeing as though it was a beautiful night, but the mechanic in him took over and he walked to the tow truck parked in his driveway instead. Within five minutes he was pulling up to his sister’s house to see a black BMW in the driveway and Rebekah and another woman standing next to it.

“Hey Zeke,” Rebekah smiled as he approached them. “This is Claire. Claire, this is my brother Ezekiel.”

“Zeke,” he corrected her and offered his hand to the gorgeous blonde woman in front of him. He noted her apprehension as she looked down at his hand. It was dark but not so dark he would miss the slight twist of her lips as she barely shook his hand and pulled it away.

Snob, he thought to himself. Another rich pampered housewife who looks down their noses at the *help.*

"I'm so sorry to get you out so late," Claire said. "I don't know what's wrong with it. It's only a couple of years old and I've never had a problem with it."

Brent had bought her the car after they moved in together. She was more than happy to drive her old car or take the bus, but Brent insisted that it wouldn't look good for *his* girl to be in anything other than a luxury car. He'd driven it home and handed her the keys. He'd said it was a base model but it would do for her. It was more than she needed… much more, but over the next few months she grew to enjoy the supple leather seats and the way the car handled. It was a dream to drive and small enough that she could even parallel park it in the city.

"Pop the hood and I'll take a look," Zeke offered.

"How would I do that?" Claire asked.

Zeke shook his head. "Never mind." He opened the door and reached inside. Claire heard the popping sound and felt embarrassed that she didn't know how to do such a simple thing.

After a couple of minutes, Zeke pulled his head out from under the hood and asked her to try starting the car. She slid in the driver's seat and turned the key. It started straight away.

"That's amazing," she smiled. "Thank you."

"Your battery cables were loose. Nothing major. You're good to go."

"Thanks Zeke," smiled Rebekah.

"See ya Sunday," he said as he walked back to his truck and drove away into the night.

"I'd better get going," Claire said. "See you Thursday."

And with that, she backed out of the driveway and was gone.

*****

"If you respected me you would tell me when you were going out. If you respected me you wouldn't tiptoe in here well after midnight like you've done nothing wrong. It seems to me that you do not respect me at all."

"I'm so sorry," Claire apologized. "I would have been home ages ago but the car wouldn't start and I had to get a mechanic to come and look at it. I am so very sorry."

"Did you not take your cell phone?"

"I did but I thought you'd either still be at the office working or by now asleep and I didn't want to wake you."

"How very convenient."

"Brent, I'm sorry, I really am. I went to Rebekah's house for book club and…"

"Book club? I thought we'd discussed that."

"Discussed what?"

"That you weren't going to something as silly as a book club."

"It's not silly and they're my friends."

"Your friends are more important than me?"

"Of course not."

"Then you wouldn't have gone, would you?" He poured himself another drink as he spoke.

"Look, I'm very sorry I'm so late. The car wouldn't start but I'm home now. No harm done."

"So you said," he slurred. "I would disagree."

"You're drunk?"

"I've been sitting here waiting for you to come home. I provide you with everything you could possibly want and this is how you repay me?"

"Let's not blow this out of proportion."

That was the wrong thing to say. Brent leapt from the chair and grabbed her by the wrist, swinging her around to face him. "Don't you dare dismiss me like that," he hissed through gritted teeth.

"I'm sorry," she sputtered, now truly scared of the person that stood in front of her... a person she no longer recognized. "Why don't we go to bed and talk about it in the morning?"

"I want to talk about it now," he spat back.

"I don't," she mumbled under her breath.

"What was that?" he barked out.

"Nothing," she whispered.

Suddenly her cheek was on fire, searing in pain and the room went black. She was out before she hit the floor.

*****

The sun was streaming through the kitchen window as Claire's eyes fluttered open but the pain was so intense she closed them again. Slowly, the memory of the previous night, or early hours of the morning, came back and she realized why she was lying on the cold slate tiles of the kitchen. He'd hit her. Brent had hit her - punched her in the face and she'd crumpled to the ground and had stayed there for hours.

With much effort and enormous pain, Claire managed to lift herself from the floor and flop onto the stool. After catching her breath, she stood, somewhat wobbly, and walked the few steps to the sink and filled a glass with water. She downed it quickly and then another and then cautiously made her way to the half bath. She sat on the toilet, grateful to be sitting for a moment. Her head was pounding and as she put her hand on her face the searing pain was almost unbearable. Standing, she caught a glimpse of herself in the small mirror above the sink. *Oh, God. What did he do?* Her entire cheek was a deep dark red with hints of blue. It was the size of his fist – a perfect match. She remembered every word and every detail. As she moved her hand she saw the bruising around her wrist. She could actually make out where each of his fingers had gripped her. It was not good. Not good at all.

As she opened the door of the bathroom, there stood Brent, dressed in jeans and a short-sleeved polo shirt, freshly showered and clean shaven. His lips began to curl into a smile and then he saw her face.

"Fuck. What happened?" he gasped.

"You don't remember?" she asked incredulously.

"No," he shook his head.

"You hit me. No, you punched me, right here," she said and winced in pain as she touched her cheek.

"Oh, shit!" It was all coming back to him. "I was drunk."

"Yes, you were," she confirmed.

"I am so sorry," he declared. "So, so very sorry."

She actually believed him.

*****

"But you have to go!" he pleaded. "We can't back out just hours before. They're expecting us."

"I can't go like this!" she cried. "You seriously can't think that I can cover this up."

"I can't say sorry any more than I already have."

"I'm not asking for another apology," Claire sighed as she looked in the mirror for the hundredth time. "I'm saying there's no way that people aren't going to notice this no matter what I try and do to it."

"Just tell people that you fell. You're kind of clumsy."

"I am?"

"You can tell people you are... if they ask," Brent shrugged.

He left her alone with her make-up to work some kind of miracle. Claire stared at the black and blue that covered the right side of her face. How the hell was she supposed to make it disappear? How was she supposed to explain it? She couldn't tell the truth. Could she?

No. He'd apologized a thousand times over the course of the day. He'd been drunk... not coherent enough to know what he was doing. She'd had to tell him what he'd done before he even remembered. No, she couldn't tell anyone. It was a one-time thing... an accident. Brent was definitely not the type of man that would hit a woman. So she did her very best at using concealer and every other cream she had on the counter to make it fade as much as possible. She lined her eyes a little darker than usual, hoping people would notice them rather than the massive bruise. She left her hair down, falling over her shoulders in soft waves, pushing it forward, helping the strands to fall haphazardly over her cheek. Dressed in a black strapless dress, a black wrap over her shoulders, and black strappy sandals on her feet, she added a silver cuff bracelet over the blue marks on her wrist, relieved they were completely covered and made her way down to Brent who was waiting impatiently by the door to the garage.

"Let's go," he muttered as he grabbed her hand and led her to the car.

"How do I look?" Claire asked as he slid into the driver's seat beside her.

"Fine," he replied, not even glancing in her direction.

"Is something wrong?" she asked.

"We can't be late. Being invited to sit with Philip in his box is a big deal. You cannot screw this up for me."

"I'm sorry," she whispered.

And with that they were on their way to the opera.

*****

Arriving a few minutes later than Brent wanted wasn't necessarily a bad thing for Claire. Being able to slip up the stairs and into the box without encountering many people she knew was a blessing. It only took a couple of minutes for the house lights to flicker and then go dark. She was able to hide in the shadows for seventy minutes until intermission. Brent had never been one to shy away from the spotlight and whenever Claire was on his arm he dragged her along with him. Tonight she wished… hoped… prayed he would let her stay out of sight.

As the curtain fell and the applause subsided, Greta grabbed Claire by the hand and pulled her to her feet.

"We're going to the ladies room to freshen up," she declared and all but hauled Claire with her out of the private box.

Hurrying down the hall, Claire kept her head down and followed Greta closely. Once inside the bathroom, and only then, did she lift her head. Greta didn't say a word – just looked at the poorly covered bruise on Claire's cheek. There was, however, a sadness in her eyes… a knowing expression that said she understood and sympathized. With a quick squeeze of Claire's hand she let go and pulled a tube of lipstick from her clutch and reapplied the deep burgundy color to her lips. Claire pulled the stool from under the counter and sat, her head falling forward, her hair covering her face, as tears began to fall.

"He's never hit me before," she sobbed. "I don't know what to do."

"They get overly stressed. Just let it go."

"But what if he does it again?"

Greta shrugged. "You get used to it."

As Claire was about to protest, unable to accept that that was an acceptable answer, the door opened and three women entered, making Claire extremely self-conscious. Dabbing her cheeks and blowing her nose, she returned to the safety of the box. Philip and Brent weren't there. They must be at the bar. That suited Claire just fine. She would have preferred to be in the safety of her home dressed in pajamas watching reruns of Friends, a bowl of popcorn in her lap. But that was not to be. Brent wanted her by his side and that's where she would be.

During the second act, Claire struggled to concentrate on the story. The music seemed to be the perfect backdrop for the sad scene that replayed in her mind over and over again. She hadn't done anything wrong, yet here she sat feeling the pain of his fist smashing into her face. He promised that it would never happen again. He swore it wouldn't. In order to move past the incident she was going to have to trust him, believe him that it wouldn't.

They left the theater hand in hand. Brent opened the car door for her and closed it once she was inside. As he climbed in on the other side, he pulled a velvet box from his jacket pocket and placed it in her lap.

"For you," he smiled.

Greta's words screamed in her head. *It's not the first time and I seriously doubt it will be the last, even though he promises me it will be. He'll come home with a fabulous piece of jewelry tonight and it will all be forgotten.* Here was her piece of jewelry. She slowly lifted the lid and the brilliance of the diamonds shined back at her. A dazzling pendant lay on the velvet pillow.

"It's lovely."

"For my lovely girl," he smiled.

"Thank you," she managed to choke out and then turned and stared out of the window as they drove home.

*****

For the next three or four days Claire's cheek seemed to get worse and worse. The pain wasn't getting any better either. She couldn't even place a finger on her skin without the searing pain paralyzing her for several minutes until it eventually subsided. She'd stayed at home not daring to venture out in case she ran into an acquaintance. Then Rebekah texted her to confirm their lunch date as she hadn't seen her at the gym. Claire hesitated. She read the text again and then put her phone down and walked away not knowing what to do. An hour later she made the decision to go. Brent had hit her, yes, but he wasn't going to dictate her social life. Meeting Rebekah for lunch was probably the pick me up she desperately needed. With a quick reply back she hit the send button. She would go to lunch and have a great time not having to think about anything but good food and good conversation.

That, however, was not to be.

"What the hell happened to you?" Rebekah asked as she went to hug Claire on the sidewalk, her usual greeting.

"Ah," Claire stuttered.

"Oh, hell no!" Rebekah yelled, causing the few pedestrians around them to stop and stare.

"Please don't make a scene," Claire begged.

"A scene?" Rebekah asked incredulously. "That asshole smacked you and *you* don't want *me* to make a scene. I'll kill him!"

"Let's just go have some lunch. I really don't want to talk about it," Claire pleaded.

They were seated quickly inside the restaurant and placed their orders; Rebekah a grilled chicken southwestern salad and Claire a bowl of French onion soup. Claire knew that Rebekah was itching to speak but was holding her tongue, probably drawing blood as she bit down.

Finally Claire looked up and said, "He was drunk and didn't mean to. He's promised it will never happen again and I believe him."

"You want to believe him," Rebekah muttered.

"I do," Claire admitted. "I love him."

"Promise me one thing."

"What?" Claire asked.

"If he does hit you again, you will call me and I will come and get you."

"That's not going to happen."

"So you said, but promise me that if it does you'll call me."

After several seconds passed, Claire finally nodded. "I promise."

6.

Two weeks went by without incident. Brent was stressed but once Westover Manufacturing's new product launched he no longer felt the weight of the world on his shoulders. He'd done his job by creating a marketing plan that he was pleased with, as was Philip. As long as the product sold, all was well. To celebrate Brent and Claire were invited to the Westover's home for dinner, another honor that Brent noted with pride. He was no longer satisfied with being the VP of Marketing. He wanted VP of the company - Philip's right hand and eventual heir to take over the company when he retired. Philip did not have sons to pass the family business on to so Brent's plan was to convince Philip that he was the right, and best, man for the job.

Friday night both he and Claire dressed in their finest and drove to the Westover estate just outside of town. Philip had a helicopter fly him to work every day, making excellent use of the helipad on the roof. The whole drive there Brent talked about how much he wanted Philip's life - every part of it. Claire smiled and nodded at the appropriate moments and just listened to all Brent hoped to achieve. She was proud of him. He certainly had goals and so far had managed to work hard and achieve them. But since Greta's revelation about her not-so-perfect husband, Claire was concerned that Brent was patterning his life after the wrong kind of man. She told herself that just because Philip beat his wife regularly didn't mean that Brent would. The thought didn't give her as much comfort as she'd hoped.

Dinner was perfect. The Westover's chef used to work in Paris and was immensely talented. The food was simply divine and Claire cleaned her plate with every course. She noted, however, that Greta was unusually quiet. When the men poured themselves some brandy after dinner, Claire took the opportunity to discretely ask Greta if everything was okay. She just smiled and nodded and said that all was as usual. About thirty minutes later, Philip announced that he had to get to the airport as he was flying to the Philippines to meet with one of their main suppliers. He and Brent spoke for a few minutes about work as Philip would be gone for a week and then the evening was called to an end.

"He trusts me," beamed Brent on the ride home. "I am going to be just like him. I will have his life and his company one day. And you will be on my arm for it all."

"So are we going to get married any time soon?"

His brow furrowed. "Yes. But the time is not right yet. I told you. I need the *big* raise first."

"You already make good money."

"You have no idea how much money I make," he snapped.

"I know how much I spend," Claire chuckled, trying to lighten the mood.

"So do I," he frowned.

"I could get a job and make my own money," she offered.

"You will do no such thing!" he snapped. "I need you to be available to me at a moment's notice. I need you to be there for me all the time."

"I am," she replied.

"And it'll stay that way."

Claire decided not to push the conversation any further. One day they'd get married and all their problems would vanish into thin air and life would be perfect.

*****

Pulling on her yoga pants and then her sports bra, Claire was anxious to get back to the gym. Being able to completely cover the last evidence of her bruises had reopened her world. She'd been shopping and out to lunch with Rebekah without feeling as though all eyes were staring at her face. She felt happy. Brent was loving and attentive and she'd been completely enthralled with the book choice for book club. Heading to the gym was another reason for Claire to feel wonderful.

Brent had been watching the news before he'd left for work. There was a financial show on that he tried to catch as often as possible. He liked to feel as though he had his thumb on the pulse of the market. He read the Wall Street journal and the New York Times every day at work too. He hadn't turned off the TV before he left and the hum of the entertainment news kept Claire company as she brushed her hair and wrapped it around her fingers in a bun and secured it with two long wooden sticks. As she sat down on the bench at the end of their bed to put on her shoes and socks she froze as the news anchor broadcasted the breaking news. Greta Westover had been found dead in the early hours of the morning by a hotel groundskeeper. An apparent suicide, Ms. Westover had apparently thrown herself off the balcony at the Westover luxury penthouse suite in an exclusive high-rise downtown. She'd landed on the rock waterfall below. She was dead. A tragedy. So young.

Claire didn't hear anymore. There were few women Claire could call friend. Greta was one of them. Even though they weren't close they *were* friends and now Greta was dead. Why? How? Why?

With tears spilling from her eyes, Claire ran down the stairs, grabbed her purse and dangerously drove to

Westover Manufacturing. She could barely see and by the time she pulled into the underground parking garage she was hysterically sobbing. As she stood in the back of the elevator, every time the doors opened to let someone on, they wisely decided to wait for the next one, leaving her alone as she unraveled. Bursting into Brent's office, he looked up in complete surprise and then his eyes turned dark and anger set in. He was in a meeting. There were four pairs of eyes piercing through her but she didn't care. She needed to feel the warmth of his arms around her as she mourned the death of her friend.

"What in God's name is wrong with you?" Brent demanded.

"Greta's dead," she sobbed.

"I know. Pull yourself together." He turned to the three men sitting in his office. "If you could give us a minute?"

They quickly gathered their folders and papers and escaped before another scene took place. Now, with the door closed, Claire threw herself into Brent's arms, wailing in despair.

"Seriously!" he snapped. "Stop it!" He pushed her away and pulled a handkerchief from his pocket. "Blow your nose and stop this incessant blubbering."

"Greta threw herself off a balcony, plunging to her death. She was my friend and I'm sad she'd gone."

"Greta was a selfish bitch who has made a mess of Philip's life. He's having to cut his meetings in the Philippines short to come home and deal with this mess. You would think she could have at least waited 'til it was convenient."

The callousness of his voice sent shivers up Claire's spine. The coldness of his tone told her she would find no comfort here.

"And do you think it is appropriate to arrive here dressed like that?" he snarled as he looked her over from head to toe. "I took you out of the trailer park. Dress like it."

"I'm sorry," she mumbled as she blew her nose again. "I'll let you get back to your meeting."

As she walked through the doorway she heard him say, "I'll make your apologies for your behavior. Make sure it never happens again. I have an image to uphold. You can't keep embarrassing me like this." She kept on walking.

Once back at home, Claire flung herself on her bed and cried 'til she had no tears left. Her nose was raw and her eyes stung. She showered, dressed in an outfit of cream dress slacks and a brown paisley silk blouse - something Brent would approve of - and called Rebekah. She was at work but took her fifteen minute break and slipped into the women's bathroom for some privacy.

It was just what Claire needed; a warm shoulder to cry on, even if it was over the phone. She thanked Rebekah for being there for her and Rebekah told her to call any time she needed to talk.

Claire walked downstairs to find their personal chef preparing the evening meal. Penne pasta with a rich meat marina sauce. All Claire could see was blood. Greta's blood. She wasn't hungry. That just made Brent mad.

He came home and changed into jeans and a polo and summoned Claire for dinner.

"I'm not hungry," she replied, curled in the corner of the sofa.

"Come and eat and stop being so fucking dramatic!"

"Ah, sir," the chef interrupted. "Everything is on the table and dessert is in the fridge. I'll see you tomorrow."

And with that he escaped quickly.

"It *is* dramatic," Claire said once the door had clicked shut behind their chef. "Greta died. She was so miserable that she threw herself off a high-rise building. She obviously was so scared of her husband that she waited until he was half way around the world before she did it. I think that's pretty dramatic."

"And how does that affect *you*?" he sneered. "Is your life going to be any different now that she's dead? Tell me."

Claire just stared at him. She couldn't believe her ears. How could he be so... so unaffected? "It makes me sad that she was so miserable that she saw suicide as the only way out."

Brent rolled his eyes. "See? It doesn't affect you. Come and eat."

"I'm not hungry. Go ahead without me."

"I said come and eat," he growled as he stomped towards her. He grabbed her arm and yanked her from the couch.

"Ow! You're hurting me."

"Then do as your fucking told." He threw her at the dining room table and she stumbled on the area rug. Tripping, she landed head first into the table corner with a loud thud.

"Ahhh," she cried as she slumped to the floor.

"For God's sake," Brent muttered as he stepped over her. "Always with the drama. And didn't I say you were clumsy?" He sat down and began dishing the pasta onto his plate.

Swallowing the sobs that threatened to escape, Claire pulled herself onto the chair and took the bowl as Brent offered it to her.

"See?" he asked. "That's not so hard."

She scooped a spoonful of penne onto her plate and pretended to eat 'til Brent had finished his second helping and went to watch CNN in his office while checking his email. Once he was upstairs, Claire let herself cry and gently touch the goose egg forming on her forehead. The only good thing about this injury was that she could, in truth, say she'd tripped.

*****

It was a somber event. The social elite filled the pews of the grand old church to say goodbye to Greta. Claire stood next to Brent, her hand in his, feeling the beginnings of despair that she imagined to have plagued Greta. A wide-brimmed black hat covered the blue bump on her forehead and dark glasses hid her bloodshot eyes. She wore a conservative, yet fashionable, black knee-length dress and black pumps. Brent couldn't fault her appearance, nor her behavior. She was on display and she played her part well. Well enough until she heard Philip say to Brent, "This is damn inconvenient. I have to stay here for the next week while Greta's family is here. It puts the negotiations with the factory on hold for nearly two weeks before I can get back there. If she's screwed this deal for me, I'll…"

"You'll what?" Claire asked, taking a step closer. "She's already dead. What more can you do to her?"

Brent glared at her and the message was received loud and clear. "I'm going to take a seat," she cowered and turned and walked to the pew reserved for Philip's close family and friends.

When they returned home later that morning, they hadn't even made it through the door before Brent let her have it with both barrels.

"How dare you speak to Philip that way? How dare you accuse him of anything while standing at her funeral? How dare you make me look bad? Are you trying to sabotage my career?" He was seething.

"What happened to us?"

"What?"

"We used to be so happy and we relished every moment together. I gave up everything to be with you because I loved you. We were happy, weren't we? It wasn't just my imagination, was it?"

"What are you fucking going on about? Nothing has changed."

"I'm going to get changed."

"I'm going to work," he yelled as he headed back to the garage door. "I'll see you tonight."

Claire continued up the stairs and into her walk-in closet. She looked at all of the sequins and silks and beautiful things that were hanging all around her. Her rack of shoes had been her pride and joy. Was it all worth it? Was she willing to live the life Brent demanded of her in order to wear pretty things and drive a nice car?

*****

Bethany had been Claire's best friend since 3rd grade. They lived on the same block and walked to and from school together every day. They suffered through the transition to middle school, dealing with the seemingly never-ending pubescent years and finally coming into their own at the end of 8th grade.

While Claire was long-legged, blonde and beautiful, Bethany was short, stumpy, and had braces and frizzy dull brown hair. What she lacked in physical appeal, she made up with spunk, personality, and loyalty. There wasn't anyone else that Claire confided in. Bethany was her rock.

Two weeks before their 9th grade began, they sat in Claire's bedroom trying to decide what classes to take. The goal was to get through the required classes as quickly as possible so they could relax and enjoy their senior year taking basket weaving and yoga. With their core classes picked they had to find a P.E. class and one more elective.

"How about weight lifting?" Bethany suggested.

"You've got to be kidding, right?" shot back Claire. "I can't even lift a sack of potatoes."

"Then it'd be good for you," Bethany grinned. "Okay, so no weightlifting. How about skiing?"

"Skiing? I love the snow," replied Claire.

"Guess what? We'd get excused every Wednesday to go to the ski resort. That is seriously cool!"

"I think we've found our P.E. class!"

"Let's see," Bethany continued as she read through the description. "You don't have to know how to ski. That means we're in," she laughed. "The equipment will be supplied and the fees are $200 for the semester."

"Let me go and check with Mom," Claire said as she jumped from her bed and hurried out to look for her mother.

After filling her in on the plan, Claire's mom just frowned and shook her head. "There's no way you can take skiing. We just don't have the money to pay that kind of fee. Your classes will have to be ones included in the standard fee. There's no money to pay for anything else."

"But, mom," Claire protested. "It's not fair!"

"I know and I'm sorry but that's just the way it is. Find another class."

Claire stomped back to her room, Bethany obviously having heard the exchange between mother and daughter.

"You know what? Let's just do badminton. How hard can

that be?" Bethany smiled. "We can try for skiing our senior year."

So badminton it would be. Another disappointment for Claire. She hated being poor.

*****

A large bouquet of flowers were in Brent's hands as he walked into the kitchen. He placed them on the counter in front of Claire and looked remorseful.

"I'm sorry about earlier. I was wrong to speak to you like that. I'm sure it is hard for you to have a friend die and I should be more sensitive. It's just that it's so stressful at the office and Philip wants to talk to someone and he's chosen me so I'm hearing another side to Greta that perhaps you weren't aware of. You know she wasn't very nice to him all the time. But let's not talk about that now. I'm sorry and I hope you can forgive me."

"Of course," Claire smiled and walked into his outstretched arms. "I love you." No. Claire never wanted to be poor again and being with Brent would ensure that.

7.

"What the hell happened to you? Did that bastard hit you again?" Rebekah asked when they met for lunch the next day.

"No, nothing like that," Claire said, telling herself he hadn't hit her at all. She'd tripped, after he shoved her, but she wouldn't reveal that to Rebekah. "I had one of my clumsy moments and tripped on the area rug. Fortunately the dining room table was there to break my fall."

"Damn, girl! Are you sure that's what really happened?" Rebekah didn't look at all convinced.

"Really," she insisted. "I really did trip on the rug. You should have seen it a couple of days ago."

"You would tell me if it was something else, wouldn't you?"

"Of course I would," Claire assured her. "But it really was all very innocent," she lied, hoping Rebekah would let it drop.

Was this how it started for Greta? Was Philip once loving and kind and then one day, out of the blue, taking her completely by surprise, hit her for the first time? Was she constantly on edge waiting for the second time to happen? Did she tell herself it was probably her fault that he'd lashed out at her with his fist? That she was to blame?

The waiter took their orders and Rebekah began telling the most hysterical story about one of the lawyers in her firm and a company party where he'd gotten completely wasted and stripped down to his underwear and sang Rudolph, only it wasn't his nose that glowed. Claire laughed in all the right places and when it came time to pay the bill, she pulled her black American Express from her Gucci wallet and took care of the whole thing, prompting Rebekah to thank her several times over. Yes, there were lots of benefits to not being poor. But how much should one give up for financial security?

That was the question that haunted her waking hours for the next several days as she went about her normal routine. She shopped for a new dress for a fundraiser that was coming up the following month. She took clothes to the dry cleaners and had her car detailed. She picked out a lovely pair of earrings for Brent's mother for her birthday gift and, after receiving Brent's approval, had them shipped off to arrive in plenty of time of the big day. The carpet cleaners came and Claire paid them when they left and was pleased with their work.

Brent was back to his usual jovial self too. It seemed as though the worst of the stress was over. He even had her meet him for lunch, just like they used to do when they were first dating. Claire's bruises healed and there was no longer any physical evidence that they'd ever been there and she'd even almost forgotten about it until one evening as they were getting ready for bed, he suddenly reached for her. She jumped backwards and slumped into the corner of the bathroom, between the toilet and the wall.

"What the hell are you doing?" Brent said, his voice slightly raised and a look of confusion on his face. "Don't you want a kiss goodnight?"

Embarrassed and not wanting to make him mad, she laughed nervously and told him she thought she saw a spider above his head, hanging from the ceiling.

"Never fear," he replied gallantly, puffing out his chest and pretending to hold a sword in the air. "Your champion will save you." He looked for nearly ten minutes before telling her she must have imagined the whole thing.

"Maybe," she mumbled as she climbed into bed.

That night her dreams were anything but peaceful. They were more like memories of Brent's fist connecting with her cheek. She barely slept and several times woke up from a restless sleep with tears soaking her cheeks and the pillow. In time, she told herself, she would forget and not be scared of him anymore. After all, he'd only hit her once.

*****

Philip Westover had buried his third wife. Greta had been a lively and energetic young woman only to have her flame extinguished by a man who needed to wield control as much as he needed oxygen to breathe. Sadly, Greta had seen no escape to the life she found herself in. She was tired of hurting; tired of being afraid; tired of living in a world of inexplicable uncertainty day after day. But to hear Philip talk about his wife, Brent was utterly convinced that she was a conniving and manipulative bitch whose only goal in life was to make her husband's life miserable. And because Brent idolized Philip to an unhealthy extent, he believed every word that spilled from his lips.

Claire knew of Brent's idol worship of his boss and mentor. She knew that Philip only had to say "jump" and Brent would do anything he asked. It scared her… more than she cared to admit, even to herself. Once again, when Brent came home from work with presents she pushed her fear to the far recesses of her mind.

"It's been so crazy and we've hardly seen each other so I thought this would be good for us," he said as he handed Claire a brochure. He was excited and anxious for her reaction.

"What is it?"

"Open it and take a look!" he urged.

Seven days in Italy. They would stay in five-star hotels while touring the country.

"Just you and me, babe."

Claire smiled. "That sounds heavenly. When do we leave?"

"Friday morning."

"This Friday?"

He nodded.

"Oh."

"What it is? There isn't anything that could be more important than time with me!"

"No, of course not," she smiled. "It sounds wonderful. Thank you." She hugged him tightly and tried to push the disappointment of missing book club from her mind.

*****

"Italy?" Rebekah screeched into the phone. "Damn girl! I'm so jealous."

"Well, let me know what book you pick for next month," Claire asked. "I'll be back for next month's *meeting*," she giggled.

"Sure. But Italy! How awesome."

Claire should have been over the moon excited. She pulled her Louis Vuitton luggage set from the closet and began the task of deciding what to wear. She had so many beautiful things the decision was hard.

"Just pack light," Brent said as he walked into her closet. "I'll buy you the newest fashion while we are there. After all, isn't Milan the fashion capital of the world?" he grinned.

"Don't tell Paris, or London, or New York that," she

laughed. "But really? Pack light?"

"Only the very best for my girl," he gushed as he grabbed her around the waist and spun her around. "And no nighties either. You won't be needing clothes," he winked and pressed his lips to hers. "You have to look like a million bucks when you're on my arm," he added. "All the women will want to be you."

"Okay," she frowned. "I'll pack light."

"What's that face for? You ought to be dancing off the walls. I'm taking you to fucking Italy!"

"I am excited," she replied, adding a big smile. "I just have no idea what to pack now that my choices are limited… on this end of the trip," she chuckled.

"Oh," he sighed. "I'll leave you to it then." He smacked her on the ass and left her to finish her packing.

He could go from playful and loving to cold and livid in a split second, his eyes changing from a brilliant blue to almost black in an instant. It kept her on edge constantly. As long as she said and did the right things all was well. She had to remember to be on her best behavior when she was in his company.

*****

They were treated like royalty. After watching the royal wedding of Kate and William, Claire had often wondered what it would be like to be a princess. Her trip to Italy gave her a small glimpse into that world. They were fawned over, gushed over, waited on hand and foot, and were treated with the very best money could buy. The suites they slept in had hosted celebrities, actors, sports heroes, and even a prince or two. Restaurants seated them at the best tables and when they arrived at the fashion houses Brent's secretary had made appointments with, they were given private shows and Claire was fitted in some of the most luxurious fabrics she'd ever worn. She left with boxes and bags of the most beautiful clothes and couldn't wait to get home and wear them as soon as possible. She knew the fairytale would come to an end sooner rather than later but she was going to enjoy every minute she had. After all, how often would this happen in her lifetime?

She slept most of the way home, exhausted from all the shopping, eating, and sight-seeing. It had been magical and Brent had been as loving as he'd ever been. Maybe this was the start of a new beginning for them. As she laced her fingers with his in the backseat of the limo that was driving them home from the airport, she leaned on his shoulder and sighed.

"Was it the best trip you've ever been on?" he asked.

"Oh yes. There is only thing that could have made it better."

"What's that?" he asked, turning to face her, curiosity written all over his face.

"If it'd been our honeymoon," she smiled.

She felt him change before his expression hardened. His back straightened and his muscles tensed. She'd angered him.

He released her hand and pushed her off him and Claire watched in fear as his fist clenched.

Oh, God. What have I done?

8.

"It's never enough for you, is it?" he screamed as he kicked his bag. "I give you everything, but it's not fucking enough! You were nothing, living in a trailer, for God's sake. You are nothing!"

Brent had waited long enough for the luggage to be brought inside. He calmly closed the front door and then turned to her, his face twisted into something ugly. Claire had backed herself into the corner of the living room, a wingback chair between them. She knew it wouldn't stop him, but it gave her a semblance of safety. It didn't last long though.

"You had nothing 'til I came along! You are *nothing* without me," he repeated. "You should remember that." His teeth were gritted and eyes squinted. She saw his hands opening and fisting, opening and clenching once more.

"Claire, come here," he hissed. "Why are you so far away?"

Pausing for a fraction of a second, she realized it was better just to get it over with. There was no sense in dragging this horror out any longer than necessary. She took a breath and stepped around the chair.

"You want a ring?" he asked, his voice scarily controlled. "On your finger? This finger?" he asked as he took her left hand in his. "This finger?" he asked again as he grabbed her ring finger with his other hand and snapped it backwards.

"ARGH!" she screamed as her knuckle popped.

"Try to put a ring on that?" he smirked and picked up his bag and ran upstairs taking them two at a time.

The tears poured down Claire's cheeks as the scorching pain seared up her arm all the way through her shoulder. She just held her left hand and sank to the floor as she sobbed in agony.

Several minutes later, she was still writhing in pain, unable to get up. Brent bounded down the stairs, announced he was heading into the office, and was gone. It was a relief to not have him home any longer. With every ounce of energy she had, Claire sat up, stood up, and walked into the kitchen, poured herself a glass of water and took four pain relievers from the bottle and swallowed them with a long water chaser. She picked up her purse and drove herself to the hospital.

X-rays weren't needed, although they were ordered anyway. It was broken and would need to be set.

"How on earth did this happen?" the ER doctor asked. "You don't see breaks like this every day."

"I slammed it in the car door," she offered as a viable explanation.

"Ow," he shook his head. "Try not to do that again."

"I won't."

She was given a local anesthetic and then with the help of another doctor, they set her knuckle and splinted it. It was wrapped and bandaged and she was given a prescription for some heavy duty pain killers - she was going to need them once the anesthetic wore off.

When the nurse came in to give her the discharge instructions, she said, "It's just as well you weren't wearing a ring on that finger. We would have had to cut it off."

"Yeah," sniffed Claire. "Just as well."

At least it was her left hand. She could still drive using

her right. As she walked to her car she noticed that the interior lights were on. She must not have shut her door all the way in the hurry to get inside. As she turned the key in the ignition, it didn't start.

"Dammit!" The tears started to fall once more. Gaining some composure, she pulled out her cell phone and the roadside assistance card from her wallet. She called and explained her situation. A tow truck would be there in thirty to forty-five minutes. Was she in a safe place?

"I'm in the hospital parking garage," she replied. "I'll be waiting in my car."

*****

Ezekiel Dayton, Zeke, as he preferred to be called, loved his job. He loved everything about it – from the towing of cars to getting his hands dirty working on a Harley. He loved meeting new people and enjoyed the challenge of a good puzzle, and sometimes being a mechanic meant working out a puzzle. He always laughed, under his breath of course, when a woman came in with her car and would say things like, "It's making a chugging noise," or "it whirs when I turn the corner," or "it makes a weird noise but I have no idea where it's coming from." There was *always* a puzzle to figure out.

Being a mechanic was not his mother's dream for her son. Susan Dayton had wanted him to finish college and go on to be a lawyer, or a doctor, or an architect. She saw a suit and tie in his future but Zeke had other ideas. When his father hired him as a bag boy in the grocery store he managed, Zeke saved up his money and bought an old heap of rust that was supposed to resemble a motorcycle. Week after week, month after month, he worked on it one part at a time. He read books, scoured the internet and made friends with a mechanic, Jim, who had a shop just a few blocks away. Zeke would ride his bicycle there after school, a broken part in his backpack, and together they would work on it, Jim teaching his eager young student everything he knew about engines, motors, cars, and bikes. By the end of the school year, Zeke had quit his job at the grocery store and was working forty hours a week at Jim's garage and every spare minute on his bike. By the time he started his junior year of high school, his bike had been completely rebuilt and Zeke was very proud of his accomplishments.

Susan saw that her son's heart was not in any of the professions she'd picked out for him, and, as any loving mother would, adjusted her goals for him accordingly. Promising to take online and evening college classes, Zeke assured his mother he would graduate from college – it might just take a little longer than four years. He was Jim's protégé and he loved what he was doing. Within four years of graduating from high school, Zeke found himself in a position that both benefited him and made him sick to his stomach. Jim had cancer and with no sons of his own, and coming to love Zeke just like a son, sold him the business.

At the ripe old age of twenty-two, Zeke found himself a business owner with three employees. His monthly payments went to Jim, until he passed away, and then to his widow, Rita. Laura was his trusted office manager, a friend of his sisters and treated Zeke with the same respect his sister's did, meaning none, but Zeke didn't mind. He loved the laid back atmosphere in the office. The garage, however, was a different matter. He had two employees; Mick, a mechanic with thirty years' experience, and Jeff, an apprentice, much like Zeke had been even though they were the same age. Zeke was a good boss and a good manager. He treated his employees with respect and in return he expected their full attention and skill when on the clock. Even though he was less than half of Mick's age, and only a couple of years older than Jeff, they both respected him and worked hard. Gearheads, the new name Zeke had chosen after Jim died, was always busy, filling their schedule a week in advance to accommodate their customers. Business was good, but it could always be better.

Jeff usually went out on the tow calls, but every now and then Zeke liked to go and get out of the garage for a bit. When the call came in for a tow in the hospital parking lot, he jumped at the chance as it was only a block from his favorite taco truck. He hadn't stopped for lunch as he'd been working on a dirt bike all morning. The break was well timed.

*****

Claire sat in her car staring at her hand. Her ring finger was completely covered in white bandages covering the metal splint underneath to keep it straight. She had an appointment in two days to see if it would require surgery. The ER doctor didn't think it would but he'd told her that "a beautiful young woman like you won't want a crooked finger for the rest of your life… especially *that* finger!" So he'd referred her to an orthopedic surgeon for a consult.

The pain was intense, especially now that the anesthetic was wearing off. It radiated up her arm, through her shoulder and across her back. She could barely move her hand without it shooting pain through her entire body.

Why? she thought. *Why would he do this?* It made no sense to her, but then neither had the other times that he'd lost his temper with her. At least the staff in the hospital had believed her story about shutting it in the car door, although the nurse was stumped how she hadn't broken any other fingers.

"Just a freak thing," Claire had shrugged.

And now her car wouldn't start… again… the second

time in just a few weeks. She looked at her watch and hoped it wouldn't be too much longer.

Her watch. A gift from Brent on their vacation. It was expensive – she'd seen the price tag. It cost more than her first car. He'd told her that his girl would only have the very best. He'd kissed her on the cheek and she'd thought that she couldn't be happier. What a difference a few days makes.

"Ma'am?"

The voice startled her and she jumped in her seat.

"Sorry. Didn't mean to startle you. Are you the one that needs the tow?"

Claire looked up. She knew this man. *Oh, no!* It was the same man who'd started her car before – Rebekah's brother. *What was his name? Zack? Jack?* Maybe he wouldn't recognize her.

"Oh, I remember her," he said, looking at the car.

Damn! So much for not remembering me.

He ran his hand along the car over the driver's side tire. "She's a pretty girl. Pop the hood for me and I'll take a peek." Zeke walked to the front of the car. "Oh, that's right. You don't know *how*," he smirked. He walked back to her window and reached inside, making Claire nervous as she leaned in the opposite direction. He pulled the lever by her knee and then removed his arm, his hand brushing along her thigh as he pulled it through the window. He didn't seem to notice the contact at all. "Does it turn over at all?"

"No. I noticed the interior lights were on when I came out of the ER so I'm guessing I didn't shut my door? Maybe?"

"Ah, probably. We'll need to jump you."

Suddenly feeling like an immature fourteen year old girl, Claire tried not to smile but wasn't successful. She bit down on her lip but couldn't stop the giggles from rumbling out.

"Something funny?" Zeke asked as he looked around the side of the hood.

Claire shook her head. "Nope," then continued to laugh.

"Okay then. You get some good drugs in there then?" Zeke nodded towards the hospital.

"I wish," she muttered.

"Let me grab the battery jumper box and we'll have you on your way in no time."

He was true to his word. Within about five minutes her car was purring like usual and Zeke had put the jumper box back in his truck.

"What do I owe you?" asked Claire.

"Nothin'," he shook his head. "Seeing as though you're a friend of Rebekah's."

"Well that's very kind of you. Thank you." She put the car in gear and drove away.

Once home, Claire didn't have a chance to figure out how she was going to react when Brent arrived. He was already there... in the kitchen making himself a sandwich.

"Where were you?" he asked as she walked into the kitchen.

"Oh my gosh, you startled me," she yelped. "When did you get home?"

"Before you did obviously. Where ya been?"

"At the ER." Claire held up her bandaged finger.

"Oh."

"And then the car wouldn't start so I had to get it jumped in the parking garage."

"So, how is it?"

"It's running fine. I guess it was the battery."

"Not the car," he frowned. "Your hand."

"My finger?" she turned to look at him with a feeling of courage that she had no idea she possessed. "It's broken. I have to see a surgeon to see if they will have to operate on it. In the meantime, I get to wear this on my finger. Not nearly as scary as a ring, is it?"

"Claire, I am so, so, *so* sorry. I don't know what happened. I just snapped. It will never, *ever* happen again. I promise you it won't. I would never hurt you."

It seemed ridiculous to her that he just told her he would never hurt her when her finger was in a splint. But there was something in his eyes... a sorrow... regret... remorse. She saw it as clear as day and knew that he believed what he was saying. Yet, he'd promised before not to hurt her again and here she stood - hurt... by him.

"I tell you what. Why don't you go and put on one of these gorgeous outfits we got in Milan and we'll go out on the town. We'll have a fabulous dinner somewhere and then maybe see a show, or a movie, or go dancing. I know you love to go dancing.

"I'm not sure I'm up for that," she sighed. "It sounds great but my hand really is hurting and I have to take these pain meds and..."

"We'll stay in then. We'll order from wherever you'd like and I'll watch whatever movie you choose, even if it's one of those stupid Hugh Grant films," he grinned.

"That is a deal," she smiled. "Maybe you could help

me get changed into some pj's and help me get comfortable in the family room?"

"Of course," he nodded eagerly. "Anything for my girl."

With complete attention and a sensitivity Claire had not seen before, Brent cared for Claire over the next few days, even going to the orthopedic surgeon with her where they were told she wouldn't need surgery - just a few weeks in the splint. When they arrived home in the early afternoon, parked in front of their townhome was a new Audi A6, dark blue with a light grey interior and a giant red bow on top.

"What's this?" Claire asked dumbfounded as she climbed from Brent's Land Rover.

"It's a present. For you," he smiled.

"For me? Why?"

"Cuz your other car was obviously a piece of shit and my girl drives only the very best."

"Really? It's really for me?"

Brent pulled a key ring from his pocket and placed in her palm. "It's really for you," and kissed her on the cheek.

"Wow," Claire mouthed as she walked to the driver's side door and opened the luxury vehicle. Slipping into the plush leather seat, smelling that unique and desirable new car smell, feeling the gear shift in her hand and seeing that this car had every bell and whistle imaginable was thrilling. It was beautiful.

Brent climbed into the passenger seat beside her. "Do you like it?"

"No," she laughed. "I *love* it!"

"Only the best for my girl," he smiled and leaned over to kiss her on the cheek.

That evening as she sat in the family room, the local news on the television and Brent reading the newspaper, Claire fondled the key fob to her new car in her good hand. It's true that her old car had a couple of little hiccups but certainly nothing that would make one rush out and spend a ton of money on a luxury one like the car now parked in the garage. Was it a bribe to stay silent? Was it a gift to relieve his guilt? Was he trying to buy her forgiveness? But he'd been so attentive and wonderful. She thought that all the ugliness was in the past and their future was nothing but rainbows and cotton candy. That must be the meds talking she decided. She was too tired to think about it anymore. She needed sleep.

*****

Zeke stood on the porch of Rebekah's house, knowing that perhaps it was a bit late to be dropping by, but he wanted to drop off the pie plate that had been riding around in his truck since the previous Sunday - the plate he'd promised his mother he would take to his sister. He needed it out of his truck in order to fulfill his promise to his mother. He didn't like letting her down.

"Hey! Come on in," Rebekah smiled as she opened her front door. "What brings you here so late?"

"This," Zeke said as he shoved the plate into his sister's hand. "Now I can sleep without hearing Mom's voice asking me over and over again if I've dropped it off to you," he grinned.

"Want a drink?"

"Sure. Just some water though. It's late."

They sat on the sofa each holding a bottle of water and chatted about this and that until Zeke suddenly said, "I saw your friend the other day."

"Which one?"

"The one that was here and needed her car started. The rich snooty one."

"Claire? She's not snooty at all. Where did you see her?"

"I had to jumpstart her car again… at the hospital?"

"Why was she at the hospital?"

"I dunno, but her hand was all wrapped up," he shrugged.

"That bastard!"

9.

It was a closet most women would give their right arm for. There was an octagon shaped window on the end wall that held stained glass in the colors of the rainbow. It cast the most beautiful rays of light across the plush cream carpet and across the white doors that hid all of Claire's wardrobe. In the middle of the room was a four sided dresser, almost eight feet in length that held hosiery, bras, underwear and some of the sexiest lingerie money could buy. The top held wooden jewelry boxes that held exquisite jewels, along with a plentiful supply of costume jewelry for every occasion imaginable.

The wall opposite the window held a floor to ceiling set of shelves that were filled with her shoes; boots, flip-flops, stilettos, mules, sandals, and every other type of shoe one could fathom. Behind one set of the white doors was her collection of ball gowns and evening wear which would make every Miss America contestant look like they were wearing rags. Then there was a closet just for couture that came directly from the runways of New York. There was a cupboard just for her workout clothes and tennis shoes and another just for jeans and sweatshirts. Her wardrobe was extensive. Brent insisted it be that way… that she be ready for any occasion. As Claire sat on the plush carpet she thought of the thousands upon thousands of dollars that had been spent to fill all the drawers and shelves. It was almost mindboggling.

"I thought we were all supposed to dress up for the dance," sneered Lynette. "Somebody should tell Claire that she should just go home."

Nobody needed to tell her though. She already knew that she was the ugly duckling and had been for many years. Being a freshman at the high school was bad enough but adding the pressure of dressing like the rest of the girls was often simply too much.

As she stood leaning against the bleachers, her head dropped, eyes looking at her shoes, she could feel the glare of her peers. It was the first evening dance of the school year. Dances in middle school were after school and over before dinner. Students just stayed behind and wore what they had on. High school dances didn't even start until eight and all of the girls had obviously spent the four hours after school primping and curling to ensure they looked their best. Her shoes had a small hole in the big toe, her white shirt had a rip under her arm that she tried to hide with a sweater that was at least one size too small. Feeling incredibly uncomfortable she wished she hadn't argued with her mother to allow her to come. She should have just stayed home, sequestered in her room listening to the radio and looking at the magazines the library gave away at the end of every month. It didn't matter that some of them were two years old. Claire loved to flip through the pages imagining that someday she could be beautiful like the women under her fingers.

That evening she danced once, on a girl's only dance that her friend Maggie had dragged her onto the dance floor. She'd felt wildly awkward as she attempted to move her body like the others. Grace did not come naturally. Once the song had ended, she ran to the pay phone, called her mother, and then waited outside in the dark and cold until she recognized the sound of the muffler with a hole in it making its way down the road. She jumped inside before it had even come to a stop and silently vowed she'd never attend again. And she didn't.

Claire fingered the fabric of the newest gown – the blue one Brent had thoroughly disliked. Remembering her challenging teenage years made her more and more determined to never go back to being that ugly wallflower she knew so well. She would do whatever it took to never be *her* again.

Grabbing her gym bag, Claire took a deep breath and headed downstairs to her new car waiting for her in the garage. No. She definitely was not going backwards. This is the life she had dreamt of and she wasn't giving it up.

*****

"I have left you message after message!"

Claire looked up to see Rebekah marching toward her. Guilt washed over her. "I know. I'm sorry I didn't get back to you," she relied sheepishly.

"Are you okay?"

"Yeah. Why wouldn't I be?"

"Ezekiel said he'd seen you at the hospital and your hand was all bandaged up."

"Oh, that," Claire shrugged. "That was nothing - just a silly accident. I'm fine." She looked down at her hand. Her finger had actually mended pretty well. You could tell it was slightly crooked if you really studied it, but otherwise she was no worse for wear.

"Did *he* do it?" Rebekah placed her hands on her hips waiting for a response.

"Of course not!"

"What happened then?"

"I slammed it in the car door."

"Really?"

"Really," Claire smiled. "And I'm fine now. See?" She held up her hand to prove that she was in fact, just great.

"Well, okay then," Rebekah sighed. "Why didn't you call me back? It's been weeks!"

"I really am sorry about that. I've just been really busy with stuff and Brent's needed me."

"We've missed you at book club," frowned Rebekah.

"I know. I've missed coming."

"Then come! We're getting together this Friday."

"I don't even know which book you're reading."

"Who cares about the book?" Rebekah laughed. "You know it's all about the chocolate and wine," she chuckled.

"Maybe I will come," nodded Claire.

"I hope so. I've missed you," said Rebekah as she took her friend into a bear hug. "Please come."

"I will," replied Claire. "I *will* come." The thought filled her with happiness. She'd missed those crazy Friday nights, even though she'd only attended a couple of times. She missed having friends. Since Greta had died she didn't see anyone except Brent for the most part. She was certainly ready for a night of laughing. She would go and she'd have a great time.

There was, however, a little voice in the back of her head telling her it was a risk she shouldn't take. Running faster on the treadmill, she tried to drown out that annoying voice, telling herself everything would be fine. She'd just let Brent know beforehand and give him time to get used to the idea. Yes, that was a good idea. Surely giving him plenty of notice would make it okay. He'd have no reason to be angry then. Now she just had to figure out *how* to tell him.

*****

"I see you as a very important cog in the wheel that is Westover Manufacturing and I see your role growing in the future. I just need to know that you are committed to me and to my company."

"You know I am," replied Brent. "I am your man. I want to learn from you and follow in your footsteps."

"You think you can run my company as well as I do?"

Philip questioned.

"I do," boasted Brent. "There is more I need to learn, but yes, in the future I see myself sitting at the head of the table and running the company."

"You are so much like me it's like looking in a mirror thirty years ago," chuckled Philip. "I do believe that you could be trusted with all that I've built. So you are committed?"

Brent nodded enthusiastically. "I am. I am your man."

Philip turned his attention to the cedar plank salmon and wild rice in front of him at the exclusive restaurant. He appeared to Brent to be comfortable with the idea of Brent succeeding him as President and CEO, the goal that Brent had had since he'd first started with the company. All his hard work and sacrifice would pay off and he would reap the rewards. He would be a god and all would worship him.

*****

I'll just be gone for a few hours this evening and I'll text you before I head home. Just meeting up with a couple of friends. The last few nights you've been working late so I didn't think it would be a problem. Love you. Claire hit send and the text was sent. She didn't realize her hands were shaking as she'd been typing. She shook her head and looked up at the mirror. "There's no reason he'll be angry with me going," she told herself. "It'll be fine."

All the way to Rebekah's house Claire felt sick to her stomach… like she was about to vomit any second. Trying to breathe slowly and take some deep breaths, she managed to make her way across town and into the cookie cutter neighborhood where Rebekah lived. She glanced at the houses with neatly trimmed bushes and green grass and noted how they all looked identical. There was no way she could live in a place like this. It was so bland compared to the multi-million dollar townhouse she shared with Brent. It was full of character and unique features that none of these houses possessed. Yet when she pulled into the driveway in front of Rebekah's house, she felt a feeling of relief... of comfort. She climbed from her car and grabbed the bottle of white wine she'd selected from their wine cellar and strode to the door. Within seconds she was inside the cozy house and embracing Rachel and the other ladies. The nausea vanished and Claire was able to sit back and enjoy her night out.

*****

"Goddammit!"

"What is it? What's wrong?" asked Philip from the doorway.

Brent tossed his phone onto his desk in front of him and leaned back in his executive chair. He sighed loudly. "Claire sent me a text telling me she's gone out with friends for the evening."

"An evening to yourself then," Philip shrugged.

"I'd made a reservation at Don Carlo's. I guess I didn't tell her."

"Or she forgot," Philip suggested.

"Yeah. Maybe I did tell her," Brent frowned.

"Fucking women. They're all out to get whatever they can from us for the smallest price. They just use us and abuse us."

"You can say that again," Brent chimed in.

"All of them. They're just cunts."

"Yeah, all of them."

"Well, let's go get a drink since you're now free. You have some cash? We could go to my club. But it's rude to use anything less than twenties."

"I'll stop at the ATM on the way. I could use a good distraction," grinned Brent.

*****

"I really need to get going," Claire repeated for the third time. "I have to get home to Brent."

The women said goodbye and finished their glasses of wine. Claire grabbed her purse and hurried to her car. It was after ten and she'd planned on being home by now. She didn't want to give Brent any more ammunition than he already had to be livid with her. Hopefully he'd still be at work and won't even have missed her and as the garage door opened she breathed a huge sigh of relief. His car was not there which meant he wasn't home yet. It would all be okay.

Quickly getting herself into the house, almost tripping up the stairs from the garage, Claire felt almost giddy at the apparent reprieve. If Brent was still at work, which he appeared to be, there's no reason he would be upset with her for going out. She skipped up the stairs got ready for bed and sunk into the soft mattress in between the fifteen hundred thread count Egyptian cotton sheets. The wine had made her sleepy and in no time Mr. Sandman had whisked her away to dream land, a slight smile still upon her lips.

10.

"Bitch," he mumbled as he stumbled out of the car. With some difficulty, Brent managed to make his way up the steps to the front door as the taxi pulled away from the curb on to find another fare, perhaps one that didn't reek of alcohol. Fumbling with his keys it took several minutes to get the right key into the tiny slot and the front door open. He staggered inside and dropped his keys, briefcase and coat on the foyer floor and headed straight for the bottle of vodka in the freezer. He hated cold vodka but Claire preferred it so he'd given in. Tonight he didn't care what temperature it was. He unscrewed the cap, put the rim to his lips and swallowed several times. The bottle was left on the counter and Brent turned for the staircase. "I'm not going to fucking make it," he slurred as he clung to the bannister as though his life depended on it. One step at a time and he eventually made it to the top, congratulating himself as he tripped on the top step and fell head first into the wall.

"SHHHHH," he laughed. "You'll wake up the bitch."

But the three glasses of wine she'd drunk earlier had Claire in a deep sleep and was not aware that Brent had arrived home. She was snuggled in the fetal position dreaming of warm beaches, white sand, and cool blue water.

He stood at the end of the bed and stared at her with piercing, cold eyes. "All women are just fucking cunts," he spat. "Get up!" he yelled.

Claire's eyes fluttered open and she tried to see through the darkness.

"I said get up!" he screamed.

"What is it? What's wrong?" Claire panicked as she leapt from the comfort of the bed. "Brent?"

"You would prefer to go out with some fucking bitches rather than have dinner with me, well fine."

"What are you talking about?" she asked with confusion.

"You knew we had reservations at Don Carlo's and you didn't want to go so you went out with those fucking cunts instead."

His words were slurred and Claire had to repeat it over and over in her mind to understand what he was saying.

"We had a dinner reservation?"

"You know we did."

"No," Claire said shaking her head. "No, I didn't."

"Philip was right," he sneered.

"About what?" She was confused.

"You just use me and use me and think you're gonna get away with it."

"Brent, I don't know what you're talking about. Philip said what? When did you make the reservations for dinner? I would have gone if you'd told me." Her confusion was growing. Hazy from being suddenly awoken in the middle of the night along with his slurring every other word had Claire's head spinning. "I think I should make you some coffee. You've had a lot to drink."

"Oh sure, blame me. Yeah, that's right," he snapped. "I don't need coffee. I need a fucking woman who treats me the way I deserve to be treated. I've given you everything and what do you do? You tell me I'm drunk."

"Honey…" she soothed.

"Don't *honey* me! I don't want coffee. Take off your nightgown."

"Why?"

"Why do you think?" he hissed. "I wanna fuck you."

"But you're drunk and..."

"STOP TALKING!" he screamed. "Just shut the fuck up and take off your clothes."

Very slowly, Claire took a step backward. The fear rose up like bile in her throat. His eyes, his expression, his clenched fists terrified her. "I tell you what," she smiled weakly. "Why don't you get some sleep and then in the morning we can make love slowly and spend the day in bed?"

"I want to fuck you now. I've had tits in my face all night and I could've fucked any one of them but I didn't. I came home to your ugly face. Now take your fucking clothes off."

His anger was real. Claire's fear was real. He outweighed her by a good eighty pounds and he stood between the bed and the door. There was no escaping him. Her heart was beating so hard she could barely think.

"Okay," she smiled, resigned to the idea of lying on the bed while he did whatever he needed to do. "Okay." With her hands shaking violently, she dropped her nightgown from her shoulders and felt it cascade down her body to pool at her feet. Then she slipped her thumbs in her panties and shoved them down her thighs, leaving her exposed and vulnerable. Never had he made her feel like this. Never had he forced himself when she didn't want to make love. Never had she seen the expression on his face that he wore now. This was no longer Brent. This was Philip.

"Were you with Philip tonight?" she hesitantly asked.

"We went to his club."

"Ah."

"What's that supposed to mean?" he barked out.

"Nothing," Claire spoke softly.

Brent had removed his clothes and stepped toward her. Claire stepped backwards again.

"Lie down," he demanded.

She did as she was told. He fell on top of her, the stench of his breath causing her to turn her head away and gasp for air. He fumbled with her breasts, grabbing and squeezing acting like a teenage boy, ignorant of what to do or how to please a woman. Claire closed her eyes and hoped it would be over quickly but as soon as the thought came into her mind she felt him on her thigh. There was no erection, not even a tiny one. The groping continued for several minutes.

"Suck me," he commanded as he rolled off her and onto the bed.

"Brent, you need some sleep."

"I. SAID. SUCK. ME." He grabbed her by the hair and yanked causing a cry to escape her lips. "Don't fucking make a sound," he spat through gritted teeth.

Tears rolled down her cheeks and he shoved her face into his groin, lifting his hips up to meet her. With each sob, with each cough, he gripped her hair tighter and pushed her to him, repeatedly gagging. He just laughed.

"Too much of a man for you," he cackled as he pumped his hips up.

After a couple of minutes, gasping for breath, Claire reached for his hand fisted in her hair. Her head was met with his other fist.

"Don't fucking move till I tell you you can move," he said calmly. "I'm not done."

"Please?" she choked.

"Are you begging?" he asked as he withdrew from her mouth.

"I am. You're hurting me."

In one swift move, Brent hurled her off him and onto the bed and he was on top of her, although this time, she was facing the bed. His right hand squeezed her neck as he forced her face into the bed, making her gasp for air. His other hand clutched her hip holding her in place so she couldn't move, not even an inch. He forced her legs apart and grinned.

"I've always wondered what this felt like," he said as he shoved himself inside her.

"No, please," she cried. "Not this please." As he entered her, she felt the massive spasm of intense pain as he tore her open. Her hands gripped the duvet as she cried into the blanket, soaking it quickly with tears of pain and fear. Her audible sobs told her story of agony and terror. They fell on deaf ears.

Brent just ignored her as he pumped his hips in and out, feeling the tightness of her anus against him.

"This is fucking like it should be," he laughed. "You are so damn tight and it feels so much better than your pussy. I think this is my new favorite position."

Within just a few moments he was done, sated and pleased with himself, and pulling out of her body leaving a bloody mess in his wake. He staggered into the bathroom to relieve himself and then flopped onto the bed beside her, the alcohol stench now combined with sweat and body odor.

"Thank you," he smirked. "That was probably the best sex we've ever had." He was asleep in mere seconds.

Unable to move for the pain, Claire remained still, lying next to the man whom she'd loved with all of her heart and soul… the man she now feared. Bile settled in her throat and with nothing but sheer will she forced her body to move and take her to the bathroom where she vomited violently into the unflushed toilet. Sinking to the marble tiled floor the pain was so intense she thought she might be ripping in two. Her head throbbed – a large bump and bruise forming where he'd struck her and her bottom was on fire. She felt the torn flesh and her hand was turned red from the blood. Able to reach a washcloth, Claire attempted to clean herself up. She rinsed her mouth out with mouthwash and dabbed at the blood, each touch sending more pain through her body. She crawled into her closet and pulled open a drawer that held sweats and a t-shirt that she gently pulled over herself and then she laid her head on the carpet and sobbed until she fell asleep as the brilliant sunlight began to glisten through the stained glass window.

Awaking slowly several hours later, Claire listened for noises in the house, signs that Brent was awake and up, but all was quiet. Relief flooded through her and as she attempted to stand the events of just a few hours ago came crashing back. Her head pounded and it was almost impossible to stand up straight, let alone walk very far. She grabbed the bottle of aspirin in the medicine cabinet above the sink in the bathroom and swallowed a handful hoping it would help with the pain. Peeking into the bedroom she could see Brent still fast asleep. There was time. She could go.

Maybe she was too loud, or too slow, or maybe he wasn't really asleep at all. As she was filling her bag with clothes she felt his breath on the back of her neck.

"What are you doing?" he asked.

Her muscles contracted and she stood perfectly still unable to think of a response.

"I'm sorry if I hurt you, but you need to understand that I am in charge here. You are mine to do with as I please. Your purpose in life… your *only* purpose is to please me in the ways that I see fit."

If *you hurt me*? She was astounded he could say that. *He knew damn well he was hurting me. He took pleasure in it.* The thought riled her but she didn't move.

"I'm hungry," he whined. "How about pancakes for breakfast? I worked up quite an appetite last night."

As Brent sat in the kitchen eating his breakfast, Claire stood at the sink and stared out of the window. She could hear him chewing and it made her skin crawl.

"If you ever think about leaving again, know this. I will find you and I will drag you back here and teach you a lesson that will help you to remember that you are mine. Don't think that you can ever leave me, Claire. Remember that."

Claire watched the days pass on the calendar feeling numb, knowing she was trapped with no way out. She was confident that Brent would make good on his threat to hunt her down if she tried to leave again and she was sick at the thought of what he would do to her when he did. Everything about her life was a lie. Everything that Brent had promised her would never come to fruition and she realized one day while making him dinner that she was relieved about that. She didn't want to be married to him… not now, not ever. In his quest to become Philip Westover, he'd succeeded in the worst possible way.

Greta often occupied Claire's thoughts. She even visited her grave one afternoon on the way back from the gym. She'd changed her schedule as to not run into Rebekah. She couldn't face her. The shame was overwhelming. Sitting on the grass where the new headstone was placed, Claire said all the things she couldn't say to Brent. She told Greta how much he'd hurt her, not just physically - the bruises and pain would go away - but her heart had been broken… crushed… smashed to pieces. She doubted it could ever be fixed. There was too much damage. She told Greta how much shame she felt for allowing him to do that to her. How could she ever hold her head up again? How could she go on pretending all was normal?

And then she understood. Greta had been married to Philip for a few years. Their courtship was swift and Claire realized that he'd swept her off her feet only to marry her and keep her under his thumb. How many nights had she suffered just as Claire had? How many bruises and altercations had Claire not witnessed? If he was brazen enough to threaten her in public what had he done to her in private?

Yes. Claire understood the leap from the apartment balcony. It was all very real to her and sitting on Greta's grave allowed her to see her future… one she didn't want… one she didn't deserve.

When she returned home that afternoon, Claire was able to see things a little more clearly. She heard the jabs and cutting remarks – statements that had gone unnoticed before because she thought he was teasing. She came to understand that Brent's true character had always been just below the surface and now it was in full view. Maybe it always had been and she was the only one who was blind to it.

Fortunately, Brent had not come through on his promise to enjoy anal sex with her again. In fact, they'd had no sex at all, a welcomed reprieve. Brent came home late and Claire went to sleep early. It was working well even if they were still sharing the same bed.

After her second visit to the cemetery Claire knew she had to leave. It would be one of the hardest things she'd ever do but she knew she couldn't stay with a man that would rape her with so little disregard for her physical and emotional wellbeing. On the way home she stopped at the bank and withdrew $9,999 in cash. She'd heard that anything more than that would send up red flags and she certainly didn't want to alert Brent. Once home, she packed with clothes and a small bag of some of the most expensive jewelry, also stuffing the hundred dollar bills in the insides of her shoes. She figured she could pawn the jewels later if necessary and she didn't want that much cash in her wallet. Then with one last look around she put her suitcase in the trunk and slid into the driver's seat of her Audi and started the engine. The garage door slowly opened and she put the car in reverse. This was it.

*****

Brent sat in Philip's office sharing a drink of bourbon in the middle of the afternoon. He enjoyed the little perks of being the heir apparent and Philip seemed to enjoy his company. They'd spent several evenings at Philip's club and Brent no longer resisted the urge to have sex with the dancers. At least they were willing, unlike Claire. He could afford to have his pick of the whores and he enjoyed dominating them with his prowess. He'd decided that as long as Claire was at home waiting for him he could do as he pleased. And he did.

The phone interrupted their conversation as Philip set down his crystal tumbler to speak with his secretary.

"It's for you," he frowned as he shoved the phone receiver toward Brent. "It's your bank. They're trying to get a hold of you."

"My bank?" Brent questioned as he took the phone and said hello.

Philip watched the creases settle in on Brent's forehead as he nodded and said thank you and then returned the phone to its cradle.

"Everything okay?"

"I'm not sure. Claire withdrew a large amount of money in cash just a few minutes ago."

"She's running."

"No," Brent shook his head vehemently. "She wouldn't. Would she?"

"Take it from me. She's running away," Philip smirked. "She's done with you. She figures she's got all she's gonna get," he sneered. "Now she's just gonna rip you off. Seen it before. Been where you're sitting."

"Shit!"

He pulled into the driveway just as the garage door was rising. "You bitch!" he spat as he jumped from the car. "You're leaving?" he screamed as he raced to her car. Yanking the door open, he pulled her out of the car by her hair and threw her down on the concrete floor.

"Ah," she cried loudly.

As Claire reached for her forehead where it'd bounced off the floor, Brent popped the trunk open to reveal the suitcase.

"You fucking bitch. I've given you everything and this is how you repay me? You are not going anywhere. You are mine, do you hear me? *Mine!* And I have not given you permission to leave."

"I am leaving," she whispered. "I don't love you and I don't want to be with you anymore."

"What's that you say? You don't love me?" He laughed a cruel laugh. "I don't give a flying fuck if you love me or not. I don't love you. Never have. Love isn't necessary in our relationship. And you do not have permission to leave me… now or ever." Opening the suitcase he dumped everything out and watched as the hundred dollar bills flew all over. "And you're robbing me."

The tears fell from her cheeks and the snot from her nose ran down her face. She looked up at him and once again he laughed. "None of this yours. Not the clothes, not the jewelry, and certainly not the money. It's all mine. And do you honestly think I licensed the car in *your* name?" he snickered. "That's mine too. *You*, little Claire, have nothing. You *are* nothing. Now get in the house and I'll forget this ever happened. Maybe we can go upstairs and replay our new fuck position from a few weeks ago. You felt so good, so tight. I'm getting hard just remembering. Let's go."

"No."

"What's that? I didn't hear you."

"No."

"Come on Claire. You don't get to say no to me. Ever." And he stepped towards her.

*****

"No," she said with a resolve that was a surprise to her.

"Come on Claire. You don't get to say no to me. Ever."

She saw the sick and twisted smile on his face as he stepped toward her.

"NO!" she screamed. With a fierceness she had never known she jumped to her feet.

He just laughed. "This is gonna be fun."

How had her life come to this? Where was the man who'd she'd fallen so desperately in love with? How would she get out of the situation in one piece?

Brent lunged for her and she deftly ducked to the right and then shoved him from behind. As he fell forwards, Claire ran like her life depended on it. She heard him screaming her name for almost two blocks before it started to fade but she didn't stop running. Five, ten, fifteen minutes went by and she was out of breath. As she slowed she looked behind her but he wasn't following her, at least not on foot. As she'd run, she'd turned corners and run through a couple of alleys hoping he wouldn't be able to follow her. It seemed it had perhaps worked. Slipping into a deli, she stood at the window and watched the multitude of cars drive by, searching for his Land Rover. After several minutes she felt assured that she was safe.

"Miss? Are you alright?"

The kind elderly woman behind the counter looked concerned for her patron.

"Fine, thanks." Claire managed a smile.

"You don't look fine," came the reply. "Let me get you a cup of coffee."

"Thanks, but I don't have any money on me." Actually she didn't have a penny to her name.

"On the house. Have a seat."

Claire slid into an open booth and waited as the kind woman poured her a cup of steaming coffee. She added a drop of milk and a packet of sweetener and sipped slowly. *Now what the hell do I do?*

*****

"Take it all then. It's all we have for the next two weeks but if it's that important to you to have that new sweater then take

it. We'll figure out how to buy groceries with our good looks," her mom shouted as she threw some money at Claire across the kitchen counter.

Senior class pictures were the following day. Claire hadn't had a new article of clothing in months. Was it really that much to ask for a new sweater, on sale, for her photo? After all, it was the most important picture she'd have up to this point in her seventeen years. Instead, she ran from the house leaving the money where it had fallen.

In addition to reading and writing there was one other important thing that Claire had learned in school. Money bought happiness. She was miserable and her family had no money. Her peers at school always looked deliriously happy and they had money. It wasn't difficult for her to figure out the secret.

Her senior picture was taken with her in her best shirt – a white button up with a pale pink sweater. As she sat on the stool in front of the standard blue backdrop, the photographer's assistant ran to her with a ribbon in her hand. "This matches your sweater perfectly. You should put it in your hair." Claire graciously accepted the piece of satiny fabric and wrapped it through her hair, tying a small bow. "Perfect," the assistant smiled. When the photo was taken the photographer had told her she looked beautiful and that she could probably be a model if she wanted to be. Claire just laughed. She was practically in rags and nobody but her father had ever told her she was pretty, and fathers had to say that to their daughters – it was their job.

As she walked back to her History class Claire, once again, vowed that she would never be poor. She would never have to rely on anyone else. No one would take pity on her ever again. She wouldn't ever again need a handout.

*****

A single tear escaped despite the fight she'd put up trying not to let it fall from her eye. Having never in her life felt so desperate, Claire sipped on her coffee with her head bowed and cried. Crying didn't solve her problem – she knew that – but it sure made it easier to deal with the emotions swallowing her.

"A refill?"

She looked up to see the kind woman's face and a pot of coffee in her hand.

"I told you," Claire sputtered. "I don't have any money."

"And I told you dear, it's on the house." She filled her cup to the rim. "Why don't you tell me how I can help you?"

"Just being able to sit here for a while is helping," Claire replied.

"Do you have some place to go after you leave here?"

"The million dollar question," she whispered.

"Huh?"

Claire shook her head. "I guess you could say I am in a bit of a bind, but I'll figure it out."

"You seem like a nice girl and too well dressed to be homeless."

Claire looked down at her shoes – Christian Louboutin. Her jeans and shirt probably cost five hundred dollars each and her earrings were two carat diamonds, along with the diamond tennis bracelet on her wrist, the watch on the other wrist, and the two diamond and emerald cocktail rings on her right hand. With a smile, she looked up at the woman across from her.

"I'm going to be just fine. But, would it be possible to use your phone please?"

11.

"Where are you?"

"Who are you talking to?"

"I'm coming right now. Don't move and stay out of sight. And Claire? I'm glad you called me. I'm on my way." Rebekah hung up the phone and took a deep breath.

"Who was that?" asked her husband, Greg. "Claire? Your friend from book club?"

"Yep. She's running and she's in bad shape. I need to go and get her."

"Do you want me to come with you? Just in case?"

Rebekah smiled. "No, but thank you."

"Well let me know what's going on please?"

"I will," she said as she grabbed her purse and car keys and ran to the car.

It was rush hour but fortunately Rebekah was headed into the city not out. She made it to the address Claire had given her in about twenty minutes. It took a couple of times around the block to find a parking spot and then she walked into the small deli. Claire was huddled in the corner looking spectacular as always, until she lifted her head at the sound of the bell over the front door. Mascara stained her face and her eyes and nose were red.

"Oh, God," she mouthed as she saw the desperation in Claire's eyes. "What happened?"

The deli owner dropped an empty cup on the table and left the pot of coffee. Then with a smile and a nod at Rebekah, she walked back behind the counter, grateful her little stray was taken care of. Rebekah accepted her offer and poured herself a cup and slid into the booth across from Claire.

"Tell me," she encouraged. "The whole ugly story."

It took almost an hour, starting with meeting Brent in her college class.

"He targeted you from the very beginning. He's a damn predator," sighed Rebekah.

"I wish I'd known that then," Claire replied.

"Hindsight's 20/20," Rebekah offered. "But we can just be grateful that you're out! You get to start over."

"And how do I do that?"

"A day at a time. I don't mean to sound condescending but I'm proud of you. It took a lot of guts to leave him."

They drove back to Rebekah's house with Claire constantly looking around her for the familiar Land Rover. She hoped that he would just let it go… let *her* go but she wasn't sure he would. If there was one thing that she knew about Brent it's that he got his way. He got what he wanted. The thought made her shiver.

"You okay?"

"Yeah," she replied. "I just don't know how this is going to go."

"One day at a time. Right now we'll get home and have dinner and watch TV and eat ice cream. The rest will all work itself out in the morning."

Claire laughed. Maybe it would be okay.

*****

Chloe was the one who consumed most of Claire's ice cream. She was three years old and a golden-haired beauty with enormous blue eyes. She looked just like her daddy and had him wrapped around her finger and knew it. But when Claire settled into the armchair with a bowl of ice cream ready for the continuing saga of Liv, Fitz and Jake to come on television, Chloe picked her lap to nestle into. Claire didn't mind one bit. In fact, the human contact was just what the doctor ordered. When Chloe had had enough of the mint chocolate chip yumminess she snuggled into the crook of Claire's elbow and peacefully drifted off to sleep. Claire ran her fingers through the silken blonde strands and yearned for the life that would never be. She was supposed to be married to Brent and having babies with him. It had all seemed so perfect in the beginning - the fairy tale coming true. But the prince turned into an evil toad and the dream was gone. It had died a very painful and tragic death.

Eventually Greg came and put his daughter to bed, leaving the two women alone.

"That's what happens when she falls asleep at four o'clock," Rebekah chuckled. "I hope she didn't bother you."

"Not at all! Quite the opposite actually," Claire smiled. "She is adorable."

"She is and she knows it."

There was a moment of silence as both women knew they had to talk but neither wanted to broach the topic first.

"I'm sorry I have dragged you into this," Claire finally whispered, the shame and humiliation obvious.

Rebekah jumped from the sofa and came and kneeled in front of her. "Claire. I am going to tell you this once more and I need you to believe what I'm saying. This is NOT your fault. There is something very wrong with *him*! Most men, good men, don't hit women. Not all men are pigs. Not all men are like him. I know that it's hard for you to believe that right now but it's true. When you tell a man to stop… when you say *no*, they should stop. It's him, not you. Please understand that."

Claire smiled limply and Rebekah knew that she wasn't convinced yet. But she had a plan. There was a woman that Claire needed to talk to and then she would come to understand that she was the victim. In the morning Claire would start her journey of healing.

"Let's get some sleep. It will all seem better in the morning."

Rebekah showed Claire the guest room and had even placed some pajamas on the end of the bed.

"Thank you," Claire cried and threw her arms around her friend's neck. "I don't know what I would have done if…"

"You never need to worry about that. I will always be here for you. That's what friends do," she smiled. "Now try to get some sleep and I'll see you in the morning."

The bed was comfortable and Claire was exhausted but sleep didn't come easily. By one o'clock she'd decided that it wasn't going to come at all so she threw back the covers and walked to the window. As she drew back the pale blue drapes the black Land Rover sat right before her eyes.

"How?" she mouthed, the panic rising and instantly feeling violently sick. She closed the curtain and sat on the bed, her knees giving out. Shaking violently, she wondered what she should do. Slowly she returned to the window and glanced back outside. He was gone. Had she imagined it? Had he really been there? Claire crawled back into bed and eventually she fell asleep.

*****

"You're gonna just love her," Rebekah said with

enthusiasm. "And she's gonna love you!"

Rebekah had put Chloe in her car seat and Claire was buckling her seatbelt in the passenger seat of the car as Rebekah backed out of the driveway.

"And who is she? I mean, how do you know her?" Claire queried.

"She's my mom," Rebekah laughed.

"Your *mom*?"

"Yep."

"And she..."

"I'll let her tell you her story. I phoned her this morning and she would really like to talk to you."

Within about three minutes they were pulling up in front of a modest ranch style home that was older but well-kept. There was a Ford truck in the driveway and a VW bug in the carport. Both were red and shiny. Chloe began screaming, "Nana! Nana!" before the car was even turned off.

Claire smiled. "She likes to come here."

"We're here all the time. We decided when I was pregnant that we needed to live close to at least one set of grandparents. Greg's parents retired to Florida so we try and visit them at least once a year but we found our house in a new subdivision really close to mom and dad and in nice weather we can walk over to Nana and Gramps' house in just a few minutes. Chloe loves coming here."

A plump grey-haired woman appeared on the porch and an elderly gentleman in jeans and a flannel shirt appeared from the side of the house.

"Where's my girl?" he grinned.

"Hi daddy," Rebekah beamed as she jumped from the

car and was immediately engulfed in his arms.

"Now, where's my other girl," he winked as he pulled away from his daughter and opened the rear car door.

"Gramps! Hi. This is my new friend. Her name is Claire and she gave me her ice cream and we played with my dolls and she brushed my hair and put ribbons in it. See?"

"I can see," he chuckled. "Would you like to come and help me feed the chickens?"

"Yay!! The chickens! Are there eggs?" she asked.

"Maybe. Let's go see shall we?" He took her from the car and placed her on the ground. She immediately reached for his hand and together they disappeared into the back yard.

"Hi mom. This is Claire," Rebekah said as they walked to the front door.

"Hello Claire," Susan Dayton said as she pulled Claire into a warm embrace. "I'm Susan and I am so glad you're here. I have a fresh pot of coffee made and I just pulled cranberry orange scones from the oven. Let's go get comfy shall we?"

Two hours later after a dozen scones had been consumed along with two pots of coffee, Claire and Susan had bonded like super glue. Rebekah sat back and felt pure joy at seeing the light back in Claire's eyes. Her mother, by talking about her own experience with an abusive fiancé had managed to convince Claire that she had done nothing to provoke or deserve the cruel and undeserved treatment.

"I was very fortunate that my aunt recognized the signs and was able to talk some sense into me before I married him and began a family. I would never have been able to forgive myself if he had hit one of our children."

That was the defining moment for Claire. She shuddered at the thought of having had a child with Brent, knowing how unkind and mean he could be.

"At least it was only me," Claire whispered.

"See, that's where you are wrong," Susan corrected. "He hurt *you*! You are a very special person, Claire. Yes, you are beautiful. Women spend thousands of dollars in an attempt to look like you, and you don't even try. It's all natural. But it's what's on the inside that counts and you are also beautiful there. Even more so. You are kind and caring and smart and funny and you have the world at your feet but you can't see that because he has convinced you that you are nothing more than a piece of property. He used you as an accessory and then a punching bag. That's NOT who you are, Claire."

Rebekah took Claire's hand in hers and Claire smiled. "Thank you. I'm trying to believe that, but…"

"No buts," Susan interjected. "If I have to repeat it every hour of every day I will until you get it through your pretty little head that you deserve everything that's good."

"I'll try," Claire nodded.

"Yes, you will," Susan stated with force. Then her expression softened. "There's something else we need to talk about."

"Oh?" Claire was surprised and very curious what was about to come.

Susan turned to her daughter and nodded.

"Claire," Rebekah began. "What kind of car does Brent drive? Is it a Land Rover?"

"Yes," Claire croaked. "Why?"

"Greg saw him at the corner this morning watching the

house when he went to work. He drove around the block because he didn't want to leave us if we were in any sort of danger, but when he came back, the car was gone."

"Oh, God!" Claire cried. "I did see him last night."

"What?" Susan yelled.

"I couldn't sleep, so when I got up and looked out of the window I saw him, but when I looked a few minutes later, he was gone. How would he know where I was?"

"Greg assumes he went through the GPS of your car and searched for where you'd been."

"I am so sorry," Claire sobbed. "I never meant to bring you into this."

Susan stood and put her hands on her hips. "Now you stop that this minute."

Claire was stunned into silence.

"We are going to deal with this together. He will not get to you. He'll have to step over my dead body first."

"Oh, please don't say things like that," pleaded Claire.

Susan laughed. "That little punk can't best me."

Rebekah laughed too. "She's right. You obviously need to get to know my mom better."

"And," Susan added. "Rebekah obviously hasn't informed you that my other son-in-law, Rachel's husband, is a deputy sheriff."

Chloe and her Gramps came in the back door. Chloe was covered in mud and looking particularly proud of herself.

"We got eggs," she beamed.

"Did you tunnel to China to get them?" asked Rebekah.

"No silly," Chloe giggled. "We got them from the chickens."

"I think little miss princess needs a bath," Bill Dayton said, slightly worried at what his daughter was going to say.

"I would agree with that," chuckled Rebekah.

With relief, Bill added, "I'll take care of it."

"Her spare clothes are in the hall closet," Susan informed her husband.

Off they went down the hall, leaving the three women alone once again.

"You'll stay here," Susan stated. "That bastard has no idea where we live."

"Mom!" gasped Rebekah.

"Well, he is," she reaffirmed.

"I agree, Susan. He is a bastard," insisted Claire and they all burst into peals of laughter.

*****

"I'll give you $7,500 for it."

"But it cost three times that!" Claire exclaimed.

The first thing she pawned was the watch Brent had given to her in Milan. She was more than thrilled to see it go.

"$9,500. Final offer."

"I'll take it. Cash please."

"Fine. But I'll have to open the safe. It'll be a minute."

Claire nodded. She'd wait an hour if it meant nearly ten thousand dollars in her hand. There was so much she had to do to begin her life over and it was going to cost money. Lots of money. How she hated money.

"What's the first thing on your list to buy?" asked Susan, standing patiently at her side.

"Clothes," shrugged Claire. "I can't keep wearing the same thing day after day."

The owner of the pawn shop returned with a wad of cash in his hand. He counted out the bills and then took the watch in exchange for the money. "Pleasure doing business with you, ma'am." When Claire said she'd probably be back in a few days he was thrilled. "Any time," he smiled.

Back in the safety of Susan's bug, Claire said, "Well, I guess it's to the mall?"

"How far do you want that money to go?"

"A long way," Claire replied.

"Then we are definitely *not* going to the mall."

A few minutes later they pulled into the K-Mart parking lot. A look of horror appeared on Claire's face.

"I know, but you wouldn't let me help with buying clothes," Susan snapped. "I offered multiple times and every time you give me an adamant *no.* If you are going to do it on your own, and I have to confess that I admire your determination, but if you are going to do this all by yourself, thriftiness will be the key. And, you might just be surprised in there. It's not *horrible* stuff," she winked.

Forty-five minutes later they walked out of the store with several bags holding clothes, underwear, make-up, hair accessories and a new wallet.

"I don't know why I need a wallet," Claire sighed on the way back to Susan's house. "I don't have anything to put in it. Not even a driver's license!"

"Bill talked to Andy today. He's my son-in-law… the one that's a deputy sheriff. He's going to help you get a new license."

"But I have no I.D."

"Yep. They deal with that all the time when women have to flee their abusers with just the clothes on their back. It will all be okay. I promise."

And it was. In just a few days, they met with Andy and went through all of the red tape to get a new copy of her birth certificate, a new social security card, and then finally, a driver's license.

"Yay!! I can drive again," she cheered. "If only I had a car," she chuckled.

"I'm working on that too," Susan replied.

"You are *not* buying me a car!" Claire was horrified.

"Of course I'm not!" laughed Susan. "But I have my sources to get you the deal of a lifetime," she winked.

Claire had been with Susan and Bill for a week and each night that she retired to the guest room, which Susan now referred to as Claire's room, the heaviness in her heart lifted a little more. It was a strange feeling to feel at home with Bill and Susan. She'd only known them for a week, but they'd become the parents she no longer had. Her dad had died while she was in college and her mother not long after. Claire hadn't even realized their passing had left such a hole. For most of her life she thought she'd hated them for being poor and not being able to give her what she thought she deserved. What a difference ten or fifteen years makes. When she'd first stayed with the Dayton's she'd thought they were the parents she'd always dreamed of having, only to realize that if she'd given her own parents a chance, they would have filled her needs. It was disheartening to her that she recognized that fact way too late.

*****

"This is delicious!" Bill complimented Claire on dinner.

"Thank you," she smiled. "It's a dish I learned from a chef at a restaurant in Venice. He was kind enough to share with me his secret recipe."

"That sounds very fancy," Susan added.

"It was," Claire nodded. "But that's from a different life."

"Well, it's wonderful, dear," Bill smiled and patted her hand.

"This Sunday is our family dinner. Maybe you'd like to help me cook?" Susan asked.

"I'd love to."

Claire declined attending church with Bill and Susan on Sunday morning. She was grateful for their hospitality... for taking her in as one of their own, but she didn't feel the need to go and worship a God she wasn't sure even existed. Instead, she soaked in a hot bath and dressed in a new black skirt and white linen blouse. While they certainly weren't the style and caliber of dressmaking she was used to, they fit and were clean and she looked fine in the mirror. She blow dried her hair and applied make-up to her clean, fresh face. Miraculously, she looked pretty much the same as when she'd spent almost a hundred dollars on just one item at the mall. Pleased with her appearance, she had just been in the family room for a few minutes when the Dayton's arrived home from their church service.

Donning aprons, Claire and Susan began preparing lunch. The roast was already in the oven. Susan had taken care of that before she left.

Thirty minutes later the family began arriving. First was Rebekah, Greg and Chloe. They all greeted Claire with a big hug and Rebekah joined her in the kitchen. Greg and Chloe made themselves comfortable in the family room in front of the television with Bill. There was football on.

Next to arrive was Rachel and Andy. They, too, met Claire with an embrace and Andy quickly disappeared, with a beer, to watch TV with the men. The women chatted away furiously as they mashed potatoes, sautéed green beans, buttered hot bread rolls fresh from the oven and whisked the rich meaty gravy. The food was then placed on the table and it was time to eat.

"Where's Ezekiel?" Susan frowned.

"Probably on his way," Bill soothed his wife. "He'll be here."

"I haven't seen him all week."

"He's coming, mom. I talked to him last night," added Rachel.

"You haven't met Ezekiel, have you?" Susan asked.

"Actually, I have," Claire admitted.

"Oh?"

"He helped me with my car a couple of times."

"Well then, no additional introductions then," Susan smiled.

"Nope." Claire disappeared to the bathroom to freshen up a bit. She walked through her bedroom and put away the clothes that she'd thrown haphazardly on the bed. Once all was perfectly spotless, she walked into her bathroom and closed the door.

"I need to go potty," Chloe announced as her father

tried to put her in her booster seat at the dining room table.

"Okay, let's go," Greg said. He took her by the hand and wandered to the guest bathroom.

"Hi everyone. Sorry I'm late."

"Oh, Ezekiel! I was worried you weren't coming," said a relieved Susan.

"Of course I was coming," he chuckled. "When have I ever missed one of you rib roast specials?" he winked. "Just let me clean up. I'll just be a minute." He headed down the hallway.

"Occupied," yelled Greg as Zeke opened the door.

"Fine. I'll use the other one," he said.

The guest bedroom door was open. *Spotless as usual,* he mused. *Always ready for a visitor.* He opened the door and took the couple of steps to the sink. He turned on the faucet and began washing his hands.

12.

Claire sat on the toilet, emptying her bladder in the privacy of her bathroom. She knew everyone would be waiting on her so she was trying to hurry when the door flung open. Incredulous at the scene unfolding in front of her, she sat still not knowing if she should speak. There stood Zeke at the sink washing his hands.

The bathroom was an L-shape that fit in like a tetris piece to the L-shaped closet, making a perfect rectangle. There was a wall than separated the toilet from the doorway but her knees and feet were completely visible. She just hoped he didn't turn her way when leaving.

He finished washing his hands, turned off the faucet and shook the excess water from his fingers, then slowly turned for a towel. Claire leaned as far back as she could hoping to stay out of sight.

"Ah," she heard his voice. "Um."

She remained as silent as a mouse… a mouse trying be quiet.

"I'm really sorry," he said, his mortification dripping from every word. "I'll leave you to it." He scurried out slamming the door behind him.

"Good grief," she whimpered, looking down at her knees, the nude panties pulled tight between them.

Within just a minute or two, she stood in her bedroom, unable to leave. The humiliation was crushing and she didn't think she could sit at the dinner table and act like nothing immensely embarrassing hadn't just happened to them. She assumed he felt the exact same way. So she just stood.

Then Rebekah's face appeared around the doorway, a huge grin on her face. "Are you okay?" she whispered.

"Why?" asked Claire. "What have you heard?"

Rebekah burst out laughing.

"Get in here!" Claire ordered. "And shut the door!"

Rebekah obeyed and then threw herself on the bed laughing loudly.

"It's not funny!" Claire moaned.

"Oh, it is. You should see him. He's *dying* of embarrassment and all but yelling at mom for not telling him you were staying here. This is the best Sunday dinner we've had in years." She had tears rolling down her cheeks as she continued to laugh. "But seriously," she said as she sat up and attempted to look serious. "Mom says the food is getting cold. We have to go through."

"I can't," pleaded Claire. "Please."

Stifling a giggle Rebekah stood up and grabbed Claire by the hand. "Yes, you can," and she dragged her from the room and down the hall.

Everyone was already seated and waiting for the two women to appear.

"Good, let's eat," Bill said as they sat down.

The bowls started being passed around the table and there wasn't much talking as they filled their plates. Once the food was served, the eating began and all was quiet. That is until Rachel couldn't keep quiet any longer.

"I don't even pee in front of Andy, you know."

Zeke spat his mouthful of water across the table as he choked. That evoked a roar of laughter from everyone but Chloe and Claire - Chloe because she was too busy playing with her mashed potatoes, and Claire because she didn't find it one bit funny.

"Seriously?" Zeke uttered as he wiped up the mess with his napkin. "Claire?" He turned slightly to face her across the table. "I am sorry. So *very* sorry for barging in on you. I had no idea you were there. If someone would have informed me that mom and dad had a houseguest I would obviously have never gone into your room in the first place. Can you please forgive me?"

"Of course," Claire blushed beet red.

"Thank you," he nodded. "Now let's just put this to bed, shall we?"

"Yes," agreed Greg. "Let's just flush it and move on."

More laughter.

"Absolutely," chimed in Andy. "It's water down the drain."

Louder laughter.

Not one to be left out, Bill added his attempt. "Come on guys. Leave them both alone. Let's just shake the water off and be done with it."

"Dad, that wasn't funny at all," Rachel giggled.

"How about let's pull our panties up and get on with dinner?" Claire grinned.

"Or we should just wash our hands of this whole conversation and eat this fantastic meal?" Zeke added.

Now they were all laughing so hard there was no eating going on at all.

An hour or so later, after the table had been cleared, the leftovers placed in Tupperware containers and placed in the fridge, and the dishwasher was loaded and started, Susan cut the apple pie for dessert.

"Can you scoop ice cream?" she asked Claire.

The two of them cut up the pies and piled the bowls high with ice cream and then loaded the serving tray to take through to the family room. There was another football game on and everyone was cheering loudly for the Seattle Seahawks. They would not want to be interrupted with coming to get their food.

Once the pie was delivered and the serving trays were back in the cupboard in the kitchen, Claire returned to the family. There was only one vacant seat - on the loveseat next to Zeke. She sat as close to the arm as possible and noted that he scooted a couple of inches away from her. Nothing like a little more awkwardness to add to the day.

Everybody ate and watched football, cheering loudly every time the Hawks scored. Eventually, Claire's muscles relaxed and she was able to enjoy the rest of the afternoon, especially after the Seahawks won. Chloe was itching to get outside so Greg, followed by Andy and Rebekah and Rachel, headed to the swing set in the backyard. Susan asked Bill to help her put the serving platter back in the hall closet so they left too, leaving Zeke and Claire alone. She didn't know if it was planned or not, but she was exceedingly uncomfortable. They sat in silence, watching the beginning of the infomercial that was starting on the TV.

"Do you need some weirdo countertop oven?" Zeke asked.

"No," Claire chuckled. "How about you?"

"Definitely not. I don't even use the regular oven I have."

"How do you eat then?"

"They have this new thing here. Maybe they don't where you're from. They're called restaurants."

"Ha ha," she smirked.

He laughed. "I don't cook, but I like to eat so I go where the food is. Normally I'm here a couple of times a week. Mom likes to make sure I eat," he chuckled. "But this week I've been swamped at work."

"Well you certainly got a good meal today."

"Sure did," he agreed. "So," he began. "I don't mean to pry but..."

"Why am I staying here? With your parents?" she cut him off.

"Well, yeah," he shrugged, turning to face her on the loveseat.

"It's a long story," she whispered. "And your mom and dad are so very kind. All your family is. I really don't know what I would have done if Rebekah hadn't come to get me." Her words were so quiet Zeke had to lean in to hear her. "I was in a relationship that... that I needed to get out of and... well... I ended up having to leave without any of my things."

"What do you mean none of your things?"

"No clothes, no wallet, no cell phone. Nothing. I found myself at a deli and was all alone. If Rebekah hadn't come..."

"So," Zeke interrupted. "Where is all your stuff? Who has it?"

"It doesn't matter now. I'll never get it back anyway."

"But it's *your* stuff!" Zeke protested.

"Not according to him," she answered.

"That's crazy! You should be able to go back and get your stuff!" For the life of him Zeke could not understand why a man would want to keep his exes stuff. He knew from experience that when Mandy moved out he didn't want one thing left behind to remind him she was ever there… or ever breathed.

"I know it probably doesn't make sense to you but it's the way it is and I've accepted it. Andy has helped me get my I.D. again and your sisters lent me clothes and your mom? Well, your mom is the guardian angel I never had."

"I have a truck if you change your mind and want to get your stuff," he added.

"Thank you," she smiled. "But I won't be needing it. I've moved on. I just hope that he can do the same."

Before Zeke could reply the sliding glass door opened and everybody bounced inside.

"I think it's time to play Taboo!" Rachel squealed. "And this time we will have even numbers for teams."

Zeke groaned and Claire laughed. "Come on," she nudged him in the ribs with her elbow. "It'll be fun."

13.

"I think I want to go back and finish school," Claire stated. "I have regretted it from the day I quit. There was a little voice in the back of my head that told me I shouldn't… that if Brent really wanted the best for me he would want me to finish. I mean I'm so damn close."

"I think that's a great idea," agreed Susan enthusiastically.

"But I gave up my scholarship and my grants years ago," sighed Claire with disappointment and regret.

"You don't have to go back to that fancy school," Susan encouraged. "There is a great state school just a couple of miles from here and I bet if you went down you could talk to a counsellor and get enrolled for spring term."

"Really?"

Susan could see the hope and excitement in Claire's eyes. "Let's clean up the lunch dishes and I'll go with you," she offered.

"I don't want to take you away from your day if you've already made plans."

"There is nothing more important at this moment than you," Susan smiled. "Let's get a move on."

Within an hour, they were sitting in an office with several pamphlets and brochures and were working on getting transcripts from Claire's old school. The eagerness in Claire's expression made Susan smile.

Claire had been with the Dayton's for almost three weeks. She'd refused to go to therapy, even though everyone encouraged her to, so Susan was trying to get her to talk as often as possible – trying to exorcise the demons as much as possible. Susan was far from a doctor, but having suffered through a relationship surprisingly similar had been helpful in getting Claire to open up. At first Claire had not wanted to burden Susan with the gory details, at least that's what she'd said, but Susan knew if she didn't talk about it openly and honestly it would eat away at her until she was nothing more than a shell. She knew that from personal experience.

When Susan had finally broken off her engagement to Royce, she was a fraction of her old self, physically, emotionally and in every other part. They'd been together a year, and oh what a year it was. He'd wined and dined her in a whirlwind courtship and they were engaged within three months. The only reason they hadn't married already was because Susan's father was a Marine and was helping to clean up the mess in Vietnam. Susan insisted they wait so he could walk her down the aisle.

Like most abusers, Royce had started out attentive and kind, thoughtful and loving, and once he'd managed to get her to fall in love with him, it began. Little things at first - all verbal. He'd criticize her hair, her clothes, or her weight. He'd make her change outfits before leaving the house if he didn't like the color, or refuse to let her order dinner if he thought she should lose weight. He'd call her dumb and stupid repeatedly until Susan began to believe him.

They'd been together about six months when he hit her the first time. It was just a slap, at least that's what he'd called it - *just* a slap. There was nothing wrong with that. After all, she was his to do with as he pleased. It progressed from there until one day he'd hit her on the face and left a bruise. Up until that time he'd always punched where clothes would cover the evidence. Susan's aunt saw it and recognized what was happening immediately. Two hours later the engagement ring had been returned and Royce had been threatened with his life if he ever came near Susan again. It worked. She never did see him after that.

Bill and her children all knew the story. She'd used her story often to teach her children respect for themselves and for others. It had worked. Both Rachel and Rebekah were strong women and their husbands wouldn't dare lay a finger on them, even if they had the inclination to, which neither of them did. Ezekiel respected women, maybe a little too much if you asked Susan. In his past two long-term relationships both women had seemingly walked all over him and Susan had not approved, Fortunately her son had seen the light and they had both moved on, leaving Zeke a little wiser and a lot more selective. So selective Susan didn't think he'd been on a date in over a year.

She knew what it was like to be beaten down so far that up was out of sight. She saw herself in Claire and it drove her desire to help her as much as she could. Claire had the whole world in front of her and she was just starting to get a glimpse. It was a good beginning but there was much farther to go.

*****

"I have nothing left except the clothes I was wearing when I left," Claire squeaked to Rebekah as they sipped on coffee in the corner table at the coffee shop. "I pawned it all."

"Were you wearing all of it on purpose? To use it to pawn?"

Claire laughed and shook her head. "That's how I dressed. Brent had very strict rules about how I looked *all* the time. It didn't matter if we were at home, if I was at the grocery store, or we were at a benefit."

"Seriously?" Rebekah was shocked. "You never got to wear fuzzy socks and flannel pajama bottoms and a tank top?"

"Not if Brent was anywhere near me."

"Wow!" mouthed Rebekah. "I could never live like that!"

Claire's eyelids dropped and the pain she was feeling was evident in her expression.

"I'm sorry," apologized Rebekah. "That was so thoughtless. Please forgive me."

"It's not that," Claire whispered. "It was the life I wanted… I dreamed of," she confessed. "I was sure that was what was going to make me happy."

"Why?" Rebekah was curious. "Why was it that important to you?"

"I grew up poor," she shrugged. "I was sure," she choked. "Sure that having money and all the nice things that it can buy would make me happy."

"It's not the money," Rebekah soothed.

"I'm starting to realize that," agreed Claire. "I sit here in your parents' house. How big is it? Two thousand square feet maybe?"

Rebekah nodded. "Yeah, probably."

"And your family is happier than anyone I've ever met."

Rebekah tilted her head, unsure of what her friend meant.

"Don't get me wrong," Claire assured. "This is a lovely home and I have felt more comfortable here than anywhere I have ever lived in my whole life. It's just that the townhouse was three stories and every floor was probably the size of your house. It was big. And for the most part, for the three years I lived there I'm not sure I was happy. Well, certainly not the last few months," she added.

Taking her hand, Rebekah sighed. "You can be happy in a ten foot square room. It's not about the money. It's about whether or not you love yourself and the people you choose to surround yourself with. Although, I admit that I've thought about what it would be like to be rich but with Greg working as the maintenance supervisor at the hospital I don't think we'll ever get rich," she chuckled.

"Have you thought about going to law school?"

"Nah! I couldn't do that to Chloe and the new baby."

"What?" exclaimed Claire.

"No! Not yet," replied Rebekah. "But we're trying. And I'm going to quit my job when the next baby comes. By the time we pay for childcare it's not worth me working anymore. And with a few little sacrifices we can live on Greg's salary alone."

"Wow, that's awesome."

"We've saved and paid off Greg's truck so we don't have a car payment anymore and we only have one credit card in case of an emergency. The most important thing for our family is to be together," she shrugged.

A tear fell from Claire's eye.

"I didn't mean to make you sad," Rebekah worried.

"You didn't," Claire assured her. "I'm coming to realize that I just don't have a clue about life. Everything I wanted I got, but it came at a price, apparently."

"A price nobody should be required to pay," scoffed Rebekah.

"No. Nobody should have to go through what I did to wear a nice dress and drive a German car."

"Well, the car was nice," joked Rebekah trying to lighten the mood.

"Yeah, it was."

*****

"Mom! You can't rescue all the strays."

"Ezekiel William Dayton!" Susan was furious with her son. "Claire is not a stray and I will not have you talking about her like that. How dare you? Do you know what happened to her?"

"Yeah, I do," he cowered.

"Then how on earth can you call her a stray?"

"I'm sorry mom. It's been a rough day."

"What's wrong?"

"We had an OSHA inspection done and there are a hundred and one things I need to do to this place to bring it up to compliance and I just don't have the money. Business isn't bad but it's been better and I have to figure out how to make it all work."

"You know your father and I would be happy to..."

"No!" he cut her off. "I can do this. I need to do this on my own. After all, I've had for the shop for twelve years and I've kept the doors open. I'll figure it out. But thanks." He placed a sweet kiss on his mother's cheek. "Now, what brings you down here to see me?"

"I need you to find a really great car for Claire to buy. But it has to be really, really cheap."

Zeke laughed. "You want a great car for no money?"

"Exactly!" Susan smiled. "And she'll need it in three weeks when school starts."

"School?"

"Yes. She's enrolled at Western and is going to finish her degree, unlike some people I know," she frowned.

"I have seven credits left!"

"Get it done Ezekiel. The car and your seven credits. I'll see you tomorrow for dinner." She kissed his cheek and turned to her car. "Oh," she yelled over her shoulder. "Claire doesn't know about the car so don't say anything until you talk to me first. Got it?"

"Got it," he muttered.

"Laura?" he yelled to his receptionist. "Start scouring the auctions will you please? I need the deal of a lifetime," he sighed.

14.

All jewelry pawned and registered for spring term at college, Claire was finally feeling hope that she had a future. The next item on her list was to find a very small place of her own. Rebekah had told her she could be happy in a ten foot room and she sure hoped so because that's all she'd be able to afford.

The search began with the newspaper and then online. A portion of her money went to a refurbished laptop and a cell phone. Everything was so expensive even when she was trying to be frugal. All of her money was in cash in a small box in the drawer next to her bed. After every purchase she noted the stack getting smaller and the anxiety she felt was disconcerting, but Susan had brainwashed her to have faith that all would work out.

There were no other sightings of Brent. It had been nearly two months since she'd shoved him down and ran away. Every day she was away from him she felt more empowered… more positive about her life and what she could make of it. And when she found a small basement apartment that was as cheap as she'd seen, she was over the moon and called immediately.

"You're the first call I've gotten," an older female voice said. "When would you like to come see it?"

It was arranged that she and Susan would head over first thing the following morning to take a look. The best thing about it was that it came with some furniture, saving Claire from having to spend more of her precious cash. She was so excited she could barely sleep so when the sun peeked over the horizon, Claire jumped out of bed with eagerness and got herself ready for the day. She showered, dried and styled her hair and applied her makeup perfectly. And then she pulled out her jeans and white linen shirt that were folded and placed in the bottom drawer. She'd worn them for two days after she'd left Brent and then Susan had washed them for her and Claire had placed them out of sight. But today was a special day, so she pulled them out and slid into the dark blue skinny jeans and the linen shirt.

Claire remembered buying the shirt well. She'd found it while looking for a blazer to wear to a lady's luncheon Greta had invited her to. She thought she should dress a little more conservatively so she'd found a gorgeous red double breasted jacket and had bought the shirt to wear underneath. She'd worn black slacks and matching red Jimmy Choos. When she'd come downstairs ready to go Brent had kissed her and told her she looked too good to leave the house and promptly threw her on the sofa and made love to her. She arrived ten minutes late and looked like she'd just had a fabulous romp in the hay.

There were good memories… lots of good memories. Yet every time she thought of them the black cloud darkened them and the only memory that remained was her head pushed into the bed and him hurting her so badly that it made her sick to her stomach.

Shaking Brent from her mind, she dressed and put her Christian Louboutin's on her feet. How she ran for blocks in them she had no idea. And truthfully, she could have sold them for a little bit of money but she couldn't bring herself to do it. She could sell the whole outfit and buy groceries or text books, but she needed to keep them even if she wasn't sure why.

Checking her appearance in the mirror, making sure she was ready for the day, she headed into the kitchen and prepared breakfast for Bill and Susan and then once they were up they all ate and drank coffee and the day had begun perfectly. Claire hoped it would end that way, too.

*****

"It's only about a ten minutes' walk from the college," Claire whispered excitedly to Susan as they stood on the porch after ringing the doorbell. "I could *walk* to school!"

Chuckling, Susan agreed. "Yes, you could. But we haven't see the apartment yet."

"How bad could it be?"

But Susan didn't have a chance to tell her about some of the dives she and Bill had lived in while financially struggling after they were first married, and for Claire's sake, she hoped it wouldn't be half as bad as those. The door was opened and a very old woman stepped onto the porch.

"You Claire?" she barked.

"Yes, ma'am," she smiled. "Good morning," she added brightly.

"Hmph! Well, let's go take a look at the apartment. It's five hundred a month, utilities included, but not cable or internet. You want those you can pay for them yourself."

"Oh, I won't have time to watch TV," Claire informed the elderly woman. "I'll be going to school and will need all my time to study. No distractions like television dramas," she laughed.

"There'd better not be any drama or you'll be out!" warned the woman. "And no parties either."

Susan and Claire glanced at each other and tried not to laugh. The woman reminded Susan of Granny from the Beverly Hillbillies, an old television show from the 60's. She was maybe four feet tall and as wrinkled as a prune and she had to be in her nineties. But she was spunky, that's for sure.

"Here you go," she said as she unlocked the front door

and ushered the two women inside. "It's not much but it's warm and dry."

"Warm and dry is a big plus," smiled Claire.

It was small to be sure, but clean and cozy. There was a small living room with a loveseat and an old recliner with a dented and scratched coffee table. But it was sturdy and Claire could envision herself sitting on the shag carpet leaning against the sofa, legs stretched underneath the table and her text books spread all over as she studied, wrote papers and took quizzes. The thought was exhilarating.

To the right was a tiny kitchen, *tiny* being the operative word. In the corner was a small refrigerator and to the left was a single stainless steel sink. There was about eighteen inches of counter space and then the stove was in the other corner. There was, however, space for a small table and two stools, *maybe*. It was perfect!

"Bedroom's through there," the woman nodded straight ahead.

Claire walked through the doorway, a pocket door separating the two rooms. The same shag carpet in mottled brown covered the floor and multiple floor to ceiling windows filled one wall letting in tons of light. Despite the dated furnishings and décor, Claire thought it a happy room. It wasn't a large room by any means, but it held what appeared to be a queen bed, no bedding, a dresser, a desk and rickety old wooden chair and a large walk in closet. Too bad she didn't have much in the way of a wardrobe to fill it. And then there was a tiny bathroom, smaller than the kitchen. There was a toilet, a shower stall, and a sink with a very compact vanity. A mirror hid the medicine cabinet above the sink and there was a fluorescent light overhead.

Claire looked at Susan, eyes wide open. "Well?" she

asked. "What do you think?"

"It's actually not bad," Susan confessed. "I'm rather surprised," she whispered.

Claire smiled and turned around to the owner. "I'll take it, if you'll have me, that is."

"I'll need first and last's month rent before you move in."

"Would it be okay with you if I paid six months up front?"

It was the first time Claire had seen the woman smile.

"That would be just fine," she nodded. "Come on upstairs and we'll get the paperwork filled out and I'll give you the key. I'll even the give you the last six days of this month free if you want to move in straight away."

"That's very kind of you," Susan smiled at Claire.

Independence was just a breath away.

*****

"I can buy some of this stuff," Claire insisted. "I have a little money to use."

"Nonsense!" Susan scoffed. "I have closets and cupboards full of things I haven't used. I just have never gotten around to giving them away. And now I can happily donate them to my favorite cause – the Claire Larson college fund," she grinned.

"Believe her," Bill snorted. "She has more than enough to fund several projects."

"Well okay then," Claire agreed. "But one day I will repay you."

"You already have dear," smiled Susan. "Just seeing you so happy is payment enough."

They loaded boxes with bedding, towels, kitchenware, and throw pillows and blankets. There were a couple of lamps added to the pile, along with an old TV and antenna. "Just in case you want to catch the news on the local station," Susan had told her.

When Zeke pulled up in his truck an hour later, he pulled his mother aside in the front yard after loading the boxes and things into the back of his truck.

"I did what you asked, mom."

"What's that son?"

"I found you the deal of a lifetime."

"A car?" Susan was elated. "Really? You found her a car?"

"I did."

"Oh, Ezekiel!" She threw her arms around him and squeezed tightly. "I just knew you could do it! After we get her settled, let's take Claire to her new car. Where is it?"

"At my garage."

"Brilliant! Let's get moving then."

The old woman, Agatha as they came to discover when signing the rental agreement, met them as they arrived. She was mowing the small patch of grass in front of her house.

"What the?" Claire was stunned into silence. Agatha's head was pretty much even with the handle of the mower. Claire jumped from the truck and ran to Agatha's side to see sweat dripping down the old woman's face.

"Can I do that?" Claire offered.

"Nah," the woman frowned. "It keeps me young and in shape."

"Okay then," Claire sighed and returned to the truck shrugging at Susan and Zeke. "It apparently keeps her young."

In no time at all, the boxes and other things were safely carried down to Claire's new home. Susan helped Claire organize her little kitchen while Zeke set up the television and positioned the antenna. The reception wasn't perfect, but it was watchable. Then the women made the bed while Zeke installed curtain rods above the windows in the bedroom. The drapes were hung, towels stacked in the bathroom, clothes folded in drawers and hung in the closet.

"I guess the last thing is to go grocery shopping."

"That can wait for a bit, Claire. Ezekiel has a surprise for you."

"*I* have a surprise?" he asked. "You're the one with the surprise, mom."

"It doesn't matter," she commented. "Let's go."

"Where are we going?" Claire inquired.

"It's a surprise," Susan clapped. "You'll see."

Once they were all settled back in Zeke's truck, he drove about ten minutes to his garage. They climbed out and Claire stood on the asphalt looking at the closed doors of Gearheads, Zeke's auto repair shop.

"Are you ready?" Susan beamed.

"I guess."

Zeke had disappeared into the office and then one of the doors began rising. Claire stood still, watching, not knowing what she was waiting for.

"Well?" asked Susan once the door was high above their heads.

"What am I looking at?" Claire asked.

"The car!!"

"This one?" Claire asked as she stepped toward the pale blue car in front of her.

"Yes. It's yours, if you want it."

"What?" Claire exclaimed.

"Let me explain," Zeke insisted. "I had a tow last week for a broken down car. The head gasket blew and I towed it here for the owners. When it came time to have it fixed they didn't want to pay for it. It was a third car for them and they decided not to have it fixed. They signed the title over to me and I became the owner of the 2002 Audi. I managed to find a rebuilt engine for it and have replaced belts and hoses and a few other things and it purrs like a baby now."

"You did this for me?"

"I have signed over the title to you. It's yours." He handed her the key.

Claire burst into tears, sobbing into her hands. Susan and Zeke glanced at each other, wondering what they'd done to upset her. Susan put her arms around her and Claire responded by clinging to her and crying into her shoulder for several minutes. It took quite a while for her to compose herself enough to speak.

"It's an Audi," she stuttered.

"Do you not like Audis?" Zeke ventured a guess.

"No, I do," Claire gulped. "You're giving me an Audi."

"If you don't want it I'm sure I can find something else," he offered, completely baffled by her meltdown.

Claire couldn't compose herself enough to explain the enormous gift she'd just been given. It was beyond comprehension that they would do something like this… for her!

"I don't know what to say," she managed to sputter between sobs. "Thank you just doesn't seem adequate. But I can't accept it as a gift. I should pay for it."

"When you're on your feet we can talk about that," Zeke offered. "But actually, it was a great project for Jeff to work on because it was his first Audi. We don't usually do foreign cars, just domestic, so it was good experience and he learned a lot. I should be thanking you for the opportunity," he smiled.

Claire knew that he was being kind. And she knew without a doubt that Susan had put him up to it. "I promise you," she affirmed, "that I will pay you for the car one day soon. And if there is ever anything that I can do for you in the meantime, it's yours."

Zeke looked at his mother's rescue project standing in front of him. Big innocent green eyes stared back at him. If he looked any lower than her eyes, he would certainly come up with a few things that she could do for him.

"Ah, well, yes. I'll think about it," he replied uncomfortably. "Why don't you and mom take it for a test drive? It's insured under my business so you're all covered. Jeff even filled the tank yesterday." Zeke disappeared into the office to try and rid his mind of fantasizing about a naked Claire paying him back for the car.

"Sounds like a terrific idea," exclaimed Susan. "Let's go grocery shopping."

So they did.

15.

"I've found her."

"About fucking time," Brent cursed into the phone.

"Well, she disappeared… fell completely off the radar. Her driver's license address is the address of the police station, there are no utility accounts in her name and she hasn't opened a credit card."

"So how did you find her?"

"She's enrolled in Western College."

"Western? That's were all the losers go," he grunted.

"The semester has just begun and I have her class schedule."

"Email it to me." Brent hung up and leaned back in his chair. Claire had been gone for months without a word. He was sure… absolutely positive she'd come crawling back. He'd sat in his favorite chair drinking scotch all night waiting for her to knock on the door for over a week. She didn't. It surprised him. But he could find her now. Hiring a private dick had been the right move. It's was Philip's suggestion and he'd been right. Philip was always right. He had her. She'd be back with him within the week.

*****

"You know," Agatha yelled through the window. "You can use my washer and dryer. I wash clothes about every two weeks and the rest of the time it sits empty. Instead of hauling those baskets out once a week just bring them upstairs."

"I don't want to impose," Claire replied as she hefted

the basket into the trunk of her car.

"Well, I'm not gonna let you use my detergent. You can get your own," she growled.

Claire stifled a giggle. "Of course. I wouldn't dream of it."

Susan had been letting Claire do her laundry at her house once a week. She'd even given Claire a key to the house so she could come and go at her convenience. Claire was still in disbelief at the love and support the Daytons – all of them – had shown her. Greg had given her an old vacuum the hospital had discarded. Rachel gave her their old microwave because she was having a new stove installed and it came with an overhead microwave. Andy had helped her with her I.D. and driver's license. And Zeke. Well, he'd given her a car! And it was still insured on his policy. She knew she had to get it moved to her own but with school starting she was overwhelmed with all the time and energy it consumed. She'd forgotten about homework.

"This will be the last load I do elsewhere," she smiled back to Agatha who was waiting for an answer. "I don't have any detergent and dryer sheets so I'll get some next time I'm at the store. Thank you very much."

"You're welcome," Agatha grunted and closed the window as she shuffled away.

Over the past couple of weeks, Claire had gotten to know just a tad about Agatha. She and her older sister had lived together since they graduated from college many, *many* years ago. Neither of them had married and they had both been school teachers. They'd bought the house together and had lived there since the late 60's. The sister, Betty, had died a few years ago and that's when a neighbor suggested they put in the tiny kitchen downstairs and rent it out as an apartment to bring in some extra income. Grudgingly, Agatha had agreed and had rented primarily to college students. She didn't rent to men – only females, and she did a quick assessment of each potential renter to see if they'd be quiet and no bother. She was a good judge of character and hadn't been burned… yet, she'd told Claire with a look of warning.

She tried to come across as a crusty old thing but Claire could tell there was a heart of gold underneath all those wrinkles. She'd been alone for so long she'd forgotten what it was like to have a friend and Claire was determined to change that.

Brent sat down the street several houses and watched his girl heft her laundry basket into the trunk of a car. It was a POS in his opinion. He'd never be caught dead in a car that old. Never!

*****

Pulling up at the same time, Zeke parked his motorcycle on the grass and let Claire pull into the driveway of his parents' house.

"How's she running?" he asked as he nodded at the car.

"Perfectly," Claire replied. "It's the perfect car for me. I can't thank you enough for…"

Holding up his hand, he stopped her mid-sentence. "You're welcome. You don't have to thank me every time you see me," he chuckled.

"But…"

"I mean it. I know you are grateful," he grinned.

"Nice bike."

"Thanks. I've had it for a long time. It's my baby." He looked at the bike with pride. "Wanna go for a ride?"

"Oh, no thanks," she hastily replied.

"Have you never been on a motorcycle?"

Claire shook her head.

"Well, we'll have to fix that sometime."

"Sometime," Claire repeated. "Right now I have to deal with laundry."

Zeke offered to help Claire with her laundry. There were only two baskets and he took the larger of the two and managed to hold the front door open for her as they entered the Dayton family home. She'd been invited for dinner, as was the rest of the family, to get an update on her first few days of school.

"I've forgotten how much homework there is," Claire divulged as she piled salad high on her plate and then passed the bowl to her right.

"I certainly don't miss it," Rachel declared.

"Like you ever did homework!" Rebekah scoffed. "You were too busy partying."

"I did too!"

"You barely passed your classes, Rachel," Bill sided with Rebekah. "It's a miracle you graduated."

"Hmph!" Rachel pretended to be offended.

"Do you like your classes?" Zeke asked Claire.

"I do. I learned so much when I was in school before and then I went to work and it was so different than school. I learned a ton there so it's kinda nice going back to the bookwork after having a little hands-on experience."

"What did you do when you were working?" Rachel asked. "I didn't know you'd ever had a job."

Everyone around the table stopped chewing and glared

at Rachel. She'd put the proverbial foot in her mouth.

"It's fine," Claire smiled, knowing that they were all worried about her reaction to the question. "I worked at Westover Manufacturing in their marketing department. I absolutely loved it."

"Marketing, huh?" Zeke was curious.

"Yeah. It's pretty cool getting to understand the consumers you want to target and convince to buy your product. And even though it's only been a few years a lot has changed, especially with social media."

"Explain?" Zeke asked, genuinely curious.

"People are more tech savvy and spend more time on their phones and tablets. Facebook and Twitter rule the world you know," she winked.

"I don't have a Facebook page," he admitted.

"You don't have to have one if you don't want to," Claire shrugged. "Your choice. But as long as your business does." His sheepish grin told her he didn't. "We need to talk then," she scolded with a grin.

"What a great idea!" Susan clapped. "You two can work together on Gearheads. Zeke, you were just talking about getting more customers."

"Perfect!" Claire chorused.

Zeke agreed to talk to her after dinner about starting some marketing and Claire was beaming with enthusiasm. Neither of them saw the black Land Rover parked down the street, the driver gritting his teeth as he watched the two lovebirds sitting on the porch swing discussing Facebook ads.

*****

"That fucking cunt!" he hissed. Brent looked through

his binoculars and wrote down the license plate of the bike parked on the lawn. Then he texted it to his P.I. with instructions to "find out who the fuck owns it" and replaced his phone on the seat next to him. He'd been following her for a couple of days now. This was the first time she'd been anywhere except school and her dingy little house. The old hag that lived upstairs was going to be a nuisance though. He wanted inside Claire's apartment but whenever he was close to the house, the hag appeared in the window or on the front porch. She was getting in the way – meddling with the wrong guy.

Once he'd watched his girlfriend and her fuck buddy go inside the house Brent started the car and drove back to his empty house. He parked his car next to her Audi and went inside. He went upstairs and straight into her closet. How he missed her but she would be home soon.

*****

"It's pretty simple to manage," Claire was telling Laura in the office of Gearheads, Zeke standing off to the side with a confused look on his face.

"Easy for you maybe," he muttered.

"Really. It's simple to post," Claire repeated for the tenth time.

"I have Facebook. I can do this," beamed Laura, thrilled with the new task of posting to Gearheads new page.

"I'll help too," Claire offered. "You aren't in this by yourself," she reminded Zeke. "I'm with you all the way."

Shit! I have got to stop taking every damn little thing she says as a sexual innuendo, he thought. And then he looked at her and she was bent over typing on the keyboard and his eyes gravitated to her tight ass in white shorts just there right in front of him… just asking to be slapped… or bitten… or licked. *Dammit! Stop it!* he told himself.

"I hope you don't mind me being an admin on all your pages," she asked him as she turned around.

"Uh, no, it's fine," he stammered, blushing as she'd caught him staring at, and fantasizing about, her glorious ass. *I need to get laid,* he thought.

"Great! I'll work on some other stuff for you this weekend. And then we'll start planning your campaigns," she almost giggled with eagerness. "Isn't this fun?" she asked innocently.

"It certainly could be," he groaned.

"Huh?"

"Nothing. Laura? You got this?"

"I do boss."

"Groovy, groovy," sang Claire. "Well, I've gotta go do homework but I'll see you Sunday, right?" Claire asked Zeke.

"You will," he nodded.

"K. Bye."

He watched her hips swing left to right and right to left as she sauntered to her car. Damn, she was hot.

"She's pretty, isn't she?" Laura asked.

"Uh, I dunno. Is she?"

"Are you blind and gay? Of course is. She's gorgeous."

"Yeah," Zeke agreed. *She is gorgeous.*

*****

The note was unmistakably from *him*. It was his handwriting. *Hey Baby. I've missed you.*

Frozen in place, Claire couldn't even blink. She just stared at the piece of paper taped to her front door. Slowly she turned her head, scanning her surroundings for any sign of him. She unlocked her door and walked inside, terrified he'd be waiting for her, but he wasn't. With relief she closed and locked her door, pulled the draped closed and attempted to do homework.

16.

"Shit," Zeke groaned as he reached for his cell phone. It was the middle of the night and his phone ringing meant he'd have to work. After answering in his most professional sleepy voice, he wrote down the address and sighed. "Time to go to work."

It was nearly three and his sleep had been restless as he'd tried to rid his thoughts, and subsequent dreams, of a golden-haired beauty named Claire. He rubbed his eyes and sat up. At least this was one way to get her off his mind.

Within ten minutes he was on his way to the garage to get the tow truck. Since Jeff had been taking most of the tow calls, he hadn't been bringing the truck home. Tonight he regretted not having it in his driveway. It would add almost twenty minutes to the trip. He drove to the address he'd punched into the GPS and as he pulled up wondered if he'd written down the wrong address. It was in an industrial part of town and was an empty parking lot. Turning into the driveway, his headlights shone on a car in the far left corner. Assuming that must be the call, he slowly drove in that direction. As he pulled up behind the muscle car, two men got out.

The hairs on Zeke's neck bristled. Something wasn't right. He reached under the driver's seat for the extra tire iron and put the truck in park and opened his door.

"What seems to be the trouble guys," he said as he slid out.

"Ah," the driver said. "It won't start."

Zeke took a step closer as they two men stepped closer to him. He gripped the metal in his hand and readied himself. This was going to get ugly. And it did.

Zeke was not a small man - six foot two and two hundred and twenty pounds of muscle. But this was not a fair fight. Two brutes against just him - he didn't really stand a chance unless he was James Bond or Jackie Chan, of which he was neither. He did manage to get in a couple of blows before he was thrown to the ground though.

"She's not yours!" the driver yelled. "Give her back or you'll be sorry!" he screamed between kicks to the kidneys. "He'll finish you. He'll take everything from you if you don't give her back."

They drove away leaving Zeke curled on the ground next to his truck, the tire iron thrown several feet away. His head was thumping and for a brief moment he wondered if his leg was broken. He spat the blood from his mouth and shoved himself up to a sitting position. The men were long gone for which he was grateful. It took several minutes but he was able to climb into his truck and shut and lock the door. It took so much effort and resulted in so much pain that he had to rest for a moment before he could put the truck in gear and drive home.

"They've mistaken me for someone else," he groaned as he pulled out of the deserted parking lot. "I've taken someone else's beating," he winced. "Shit. It had better not be Jeff. If he's sleeping with a married woman I'll beat the shit out of him myself," he muttered as he drove. "As soon as I can clench my fist again."

*****

"What the hell happened to you?" Mick was horrified at the sight of his boss.

Zeke was limping and still couldn't stand up straight but he was at work on time, his pride not allowing him to stay home for one second. His left cheek was swollen so seeing out of his left eye was tough but doable, and his lip was split.

"I hope the other guy looks worse," joked Jeff.

"Yeah, you'll be laughing when I do this to you," Zeke hissed.

"What? Why?" Jeff panicked.

"Are you sleeping with anybody you shouldn't be?" Zeke asked.

"I wish," Jeff moped. "I'm not sleeping with anybody."

"Are you sure?"

"Uh, yeah. I think I'd know if I was getting some. And I'm not," he reiterated.

"Okay then. Well, enough gabbing. We've got work to do." He walked into the office and gingerly sat in a chair after pouring himself a cup of coffee. "They definitely got the wrong guy. Just my luck I'd be mistaken for the guy nailing some guy's girl."

*****

Claire didn't sleep. The memories came flooding back. She'd become *that* girl again. Five words had sent her spiraling backwards. Over the past few months she'd become Claire again, no longer Brent's possession, and five words were threatening to undo it all.

As Claire ate her toast and drank a cup of tea, she imagined all of the horrible possibilities with Brent back in her life. She didn't have to go far. He couldn't do anything worse to her than he'd already done. She suffered the most demeaning and humiliating act of all. He couldn't go any lower.

Somehow that thought calmed her nerves, stilled her trembling hands. "What else is there?" she asked herself as she washed out her cup and rinsed off her plate and placed them on a towel to dry. With a confidence that she'd never had, she grabbed her backpack and walked out of her apartment, securely locking the door behind her. She had classes and mid-terms to worry about. Brent was nothing more than an irritation, like a nagging fly that she kept swatting away. One day soon she would squash him and he would never bother her again… she hoped.

The thought was fleeting. She walked the couple of blocks to school and crossed at the stoplight only to freeze in the middle of the road as her jaw dropped open. There he sat in his black Land Rover, the window down. He smiled and waved and then drove past her… just feet from her as she stood and watched.

The only reason she moved was because a driver honked at her when the light turned green. How she made it to the bathroom she didn't know. Heaving and wrenching into the public restroom was the least of her concern at that moment. Her body shook violently and the sweat beads ran down her body, soaking the back of her shirt. Not only did he know where she lived, he knew her schedule… he knew everything about her life. The escape she had rejoiced was merely a brief reprieve. He was back and she knew he wasn't going anywhere. What did he want? Was his purpose just to torment her? She had no recollection of the rest of her day. She went through the motions sometimes even having to remind herself to breathe. He wasn't going to leave her alone. Was this how it would be? He'd just show up when she least expected it? Or did he want more?

*****

The expression on his face said it all. He was elated with the way he'd been able to discombobulate Claire with just one look. Just. One. Look. It was more than he'd dare hope for. It wouldn't be long and she'd be back where she belonged. It was getting too hard making excuses to friends and acquaintances as to why they hadn't seen Claire around. She was sick. She was visiting a cousin. She'd gone to a spa retreat. He had to get her home so he could stop having to come up with excuse after excuse.

He was confident the visit to the grease monkey by Philip's associates would do the job, but just to seal the deal, when he arrived home he stood in his garage with a baseball bat. With one swing he smashed the right headlight of his Land Rover.

*****

All day long she tried to focus, but she found herself constantly looking around her, searching for his face, even in the middle of class. If his goal had been to unnerve her, he'd succeeded. By the end of the day Claire was so jumpy that she stopped at the corner store on the way home and bought a bottle of wine. Once safely home, she poured herself a glass and gulped it down. Then she left her backpack on the coffee table and grabbed her purse. She'd promised to teach Laura how to use Google + and she wasn't going to let Brent dictate her schedule.

She drove to Gearheads extraordinarily aware of her surroundings and made it without incident. Grateful she hadn't spotted her ex, she climbed from the car and cheerfully entered the office only to, once again, stop dead in her tracks.

"What the hell happened to you?" she gasped as she took a look at Zeke's face.

"A case of mistaken identity," he replied.

"Holy cow," she shuddered. "What did the other guy do?"

"It's weird," he confided. "They…"

"They?" Claire exclaimed. "There was more than one?"

"Yeah. Two thugs. And they told me to *give her back*. Who? I have no idea what they were talking about. They said she wasn't mine and I wholeheartedly agree with them."

The blood drained from her face. She knew *exactly* what they were talking about.

"We need to call the Andy," Claire choked.

"There's no point. They were long gone and I didn't see a license plate."

"I think I know…"

But she didn't get a chance to finish her sentence. The bell rang. Someone had pulled into the garage. Zeke cautiously stood and tried not to openly wince in pain. Claire was so focused on him that she didn't see the sharp dressed man walk into the office.

"Good afternoon, sir. What can I do for you?" Zeke asked.

"One of your damn tow trucks pulled in front of me on State Street and busted my headlight. Do you know how much a headlight for my car costs? What are you going to do about it? Are you going to take care of it?"

17.

It was virtually impossible for her to control the trembling of her chin without biting down hard on her lip. She tasted blood but continued to bite despite the agony. Her eyes welled with tears and spilled over and poured down her cheeks. And then, the final humiliation, she felt the warm urine run down her leg and puddle at her feet. She stood as a statue wishing she was invisible, hoping that somehow he wouldn't see her.

"If that is in fact true," Zeke was saying, "I will take care of the damage and replace your headlight. I'll need you to fill in a claim form first though." He turned and walked to Laura's desk who'd already left for the day. He knew who this man was the instant he saw Claire quaking in terror, as pale as a ghost. It was a miracle she was still on her feet.

"Tell you what," he turned to Brent. "Get me your registration and I'll take down your VIN number and get the part ordered in right away. I wouldn't want you waiting."

"Fine," Brent replied, the smugness in his voice causing Zeke's fists to clench. "Looks like you had a little battle and lost," he added over his shoulder as he opened the door to go to his car.

As the door closed after Brent walked outside, Claire fainted, Zeke cradling her to his chest as she crumpled before him. He was out of his element here, unsure of what to do, but one thing he knew with certainty was that Brent could not come back inside. He laid her on the floor, noting the physical state she was in and verbally cursing the bastard outside. He tore of his sweatshirt and placed it gently under her head, her eyes still closed. Torn between staying with her and meeting Brent outside before he could return, Zeke hesitated for a split second before righting himself and striding out to meet the coward who had beaten the innocent creature in his office. And if there was one thing he hated most, it was a coward.

"Here it is," Brent said as he handed over his registration card.

Zeke took it, yelled for Mick who casually walked out of the shop. Zeke told him to order a new headlight for the car to which Mick nodded and walked back into the garage.

"I know who you are," Zeke turned back to Brent.

"Good for you."

"Only cowards and pussies hit women. Which one are you?" Zeke spat as he took a step closer to him.

He saw a flash of fear register in Brent's eyes before he quickly recovered and squared his shoulders. "You don't know what you're talking about."

"Oh, but I do," smiled Zeke. "I really, really do." He was going to enjoy breaking this asshole's nose.

"You need to worry about getting my car fixed, not things that don't concern you. Anything that's happened between Claire and me is private and I'm sure she'd want it left that way."

"There is something especially vile about men who hurt women, children and animals," Zeke stared him down. "It proves just how weak they really are to prey on things that are smaller and weaker than them. A real man would never do that."

"Looks like you were preyed on," Brent smirked. "Were you punished for taking something that doesn't belong to you?"

Zeke's fist raised just as Mick returned from the shop. "It's ordered. Should be here in three days at the longest."

"Get out of here before I do something I won't regret," hissed Zeke.

"Are you really stupid enough to strike me?" scoffed Brent. "I have a firm of lawyers just waiting for my call. They will strip you of everything you own in a second." With a smirk, he got in his car and drove away, leaving Zeke to watch him leave.

"Who is that?" asked Mick.

"Bad news," he replied. "Very bad news."

Mick returned to the car he was working on and Zeke hurried as fast as he could back to Claire. When he opened the office door she was gone… the spot where he'd left her was empty, except for the puddle on the floor. Panic instantly flooded him and his heart beat loudly in his ears. His sweatshirt was also gone from the floor. And then the bathroom door opened.

"Zeke? Is that you?"

Relief. "I'm here Claire."

"Ah," she sobbed. "I seem to have a problem."

He knew immediately what she meant. "Hold on a sec. I'll be right back." Hobbling as quickly as his leg would allow, he went to his truck and pulled a gym bag from behind the backseat. He didn't get to the gym as often as he wanted, but when the opportunity arose he was always prepared.

"It's all going to drown you," he said as he pushed the bag through the slit Claire had opened the door. "But it's clean," he added.

"Thank you," she gulped and shut the door.

The idea to be so afraid that one would pass out and wet themselves was so foreign to Zeke he didn't understand it. Even when he was being beaten up the night before he felt more anger than fear. He'd never been so afraid that his body would react as hers had done. His heart broke for her even more.

Now that he'd met Brent, he hated him even more. The smugness, the superiority, the condescension was so apparent that he could only imagine what he'd been like with Claire. It must have been hell for her and his admiration for her grew knowing that she'd run with nothing to her name and only the clothes on her back, so desperate for freedom that she literally risked her life to get away from him. And now he was back.

Zeke had mocked his mom for taking in a stray, as he'd called Claire. He'd accepted her willingness to help this person that they didn't know because that was who his mother was. She was the kindest and most generous person he knew. And he'd gotten to know Claire at family dinners and a little more now that she was helping him and his business, but he'd never felt any responsibility for her… until now.

"I will keep you safe," he said quietly to the door. "He will never hurt you again. I promise."

*****

They didn't go back to her apartment. Dressed in a pair of Zeke's shorts, that were more like capris on her, and one of his t-shirts, that came midway down her thigh, Zeke and Claire drove to his parents' house and called an emergency family meeting.

"What's wrong?" Susan asked as they pulled up in the driveway. She was waiting for them outside.

"He's found her," Zeke said through gritted teeth. "The bastard knows where she is every minute of the day."

"No!" Susan cried. "How?"

"That isn't important," Zeke replied as he walked around to help Claire from the car. "Can you draw her a hot bath?"

"Of course," nodded Susan. "But Zeke! What happened to you? You look like you've been in a fight."

"It isn't important now. We need to take care of Claire."

Susan hurried inside.

Opening the door, Claire lowered her head, the tears falling onto her lap.

"It's alright now," he soothed, trying to be as gentle as possible.

"Can't you just take me home?" she pleaded.

"No, I'm sure he knows where you live."

"He does," she whispered.

"Why didn't you say something?"

"It's my problem and I thought I could deal with it, but then I saw you and your face and…"

"Yeah, I'm guessing it was his doing. Now I get what those guys were telling me. Brent thinks I've hooked up with you. He must have been watching you for a while."

That sent Claire into gut-wrenching sobs and Zeke wished he could take back his observation. "Hey," he whispered as he stroked her hair. "It's gonna be okay. He isn't going to hurt you anymore. I promise."

"With the saddest eyes he'd ever seen, Claire looked up at him. "You don't know him."

"I may not, but I do know *me*," he said with conviction. "And he isn't going to hurt you again."

He scooped her into his arms and carried her to the house, struggling not to limp badly or grimace as his back twitched with spasms. He carried her down the hall to the guest bedroom. He gently sat her on the bed and told her to wait there for his mom. Within five minutes she was sitting in a scalding hot bath with Susan sitting on the toilet next to her.

"Tell me what happened," she said.

Claire's eyes opened and she looked up into Susan's kind and motherly eyes. "I don't want to burden you anymore than I already have."

"You are not a burden!" Susan scoffed. "I consider you one of my girls, so spill it, and don't leave anything out."

Claire took a deep breath, exhaled slowly and then started with the day before and the note on her front door. She divulged everything, all the way up to pulling into the driveway just a few minutes before. When she looked up once she'd stopped speaking, she saw Susan's wet cheeks and puffy eyes. "I'm sorry," Claire said.

"You have absolutely nothing to be sorry for, my dear," Susan replied, sinking to her knee beside the tub. "We are going to protect you and make sure he doesn't come near you anymore."

"I can't ask you to put yourselves in the middle of this. I'm not worth it."

And there it was. Susan had been waiting for months to hear the words fall from her lips. If there was one thing she remembered perfectly from her experience with Royce, it was the way he'd made her feel - like nothing. He had obliterated her self-esteem and self-respect. Claire had been doing a great job of hiding it but Susan knew that her lack of self-worth was a big part of the problem. Once she understood just how valuable and wonderful she was, Brent would no longer be able to harm her. There was still much work that needed to be done.

18.

"You can protest, you can argue, you can scream, but my mind is made up."

"Zeke, please," Claire sighed. "I don't expect you to babysit me."

"Are you a baby?"

She shook her head emphatically.

"Then I'm not babysitting," he grinned.

"And I certainly can't ask you to sleep there!"

"I'm fine on the floor. I've slept in worse places."

"Where?" she challenged with a chuckle.

"The floor of the garage."

"Okay. Maybe you have then," she laughed.

"It's good to hear you laugh. You have a nice laugh."

Lowering her eyelids, Claire blushed. She seemed to do that a lot around Zeke. But it was nice for her to forget, if only for a second, the horrible day she'd had.

"Go to bed," he ordered. "You've got school in the morning."

"Yes, sir!" She retreated into her bedroom and pulled the pocket door closed behind her. Zeke sleeping on her living room floor made her feel both uncomfortable and protected at the same time. If Brent decided to pay her a visit she knew that Zeke would stand between them and not let anything happen to her. Yet, she was also racked with guilt that he was having to sleep on the hard concrete floor, especially seeing as though his leg was injured and the rest of him badly bruised. He was, however, determined to stay and she knew that there would be no deterring him.

She quickly got ready for bed, slipping a tank top over her head and climbing into bed. There was a sliver of moonlight shining through the slit in the curtains casting light across the room. Claire lay in bed, eyes wide open even though she was physically and emotionally exhausted, the events of the day replaying over and over in her mind. She'd vomited at school, peed herself and passed out in Zeke's office and let Susan bathe her like a child. It was just too much. She just wanted to forget. Her heavy lids fluttered closed and she was out.

*****

There was no way in hell Zeke was going to be able to sleep on the floor. His leg was throbbing and his back was killing him, but he wasn't going to let on to Claire. The last thing she needed was to worry about him. She'd been through more than enough in the last 24 hours. He wasn't going to add to it. After he saw the bedroom light turn off and he couldn't hear any noise coming from her room, he threw of the blanket and got to his feet, wincing in pain and grunting at the energy it took.

"I sound like an old man," he muttered. He found a glass in the kitchen and filled it with water from the tap, then went and sat on the sofa. There was no way he could lie down on the three feet of cushions but if he put his feet up on the coffee table he might just be able to doze for a minute. He was tired - dead tired.

A horrendous pain in his neck woke him up several hours later. Attempting to straighten his neck just made it hurt worse. It took a few minutes, but finally he could move but he needed to pee… badly. Standing gingerly, he hobbled to the door and listened for signs she was awake. All was quiet. Pushing the door inch by inch, praying it not creak, he opened it far enough to squeeze through.

The moonlight traveled across the room and onto the bed and onto Claire. Zeke gasped as his eyes focused on her. On her stomach, her arms were wrapped around the pillow under her head. Her left leg bent at the knee, her panties were pulled tight across her ass and her tank top pulled up so the small of her back was on display. Her hair was tossed wildly across the pillows, her face hidden to his prying eyes. He gulped back the desire that coursed through him. Fighting every urge to climb into bed with her, Zeke walked into the small bathroom on the far side of the bedroom and closed the door.

She wasn't his type. If he had a type it was brunette and tall… all legs and boobs. Claire wasn't tall. In fact, if she was five foot four he'd be surprised. And all of her was properly proportioned. She was perfect he thought to himself. He flushed the toilet, hoping the noise wouldn't wake her and then quickly washed his hands and clicked off the light. As he stepped back into her room he noted she hadn't moved and could hear her faint breath - deep and steady. He walked back to the living room and closed the door as quietly as he'd opened it. He needed to come up with a better solution than staying here every night. It would be torture if he had to see that sight every time he got up to got to the bathroom.

*****

Brent was nowhere to be seen the next day at school. Claire searched every crowd, every room, everywhere for him but was relieved when she never found him. She'd sat through all of her classes and actually heard everything that was said. She took notes and had lunch without throwing it up. *Progress,* she thought.

Zeke had dropped her off at school with strict instructions to text him with "911" if she saw Brent. He would be at the garage but could there within minutes. Andy was also on standby, ready to blare the sirens to get through traffic faster. As Claire wandered through campus on the glorious spring day, the gloom and heaviness lifted just a little as she raised her face to the sun. She closed her eyes, breathed deeply and appreciated that moment. When she opened her eyes, Zeke standing directly in front of her startled her and made her jump.

"Oh. Hi."

"Hello," he smiled. "How was school?"

Claire burst out laughing.

"What?" he asked.

"You sound like my dad coming to pick me up from school," she smiled.

"You are thoroughly captivating when you smile... just stunning."

She sobered... and blushed.

"That was a compliment," he softly said as he lifted her chin with his finger. "You are supposed to say thank you."

"Thank you," she complied.

"Now, are you hungry? I'm all done at work for the day and I'm starving."

"I could eat," she admitted.

"Great! Let's go." With his hand in the small of her back, Zeke led her to his truck parked in the visitor's parking lot and they drove about fifteen minutes and pulled into what looked like a dive bar... a dive bar that should probably be condemned by the county.

Her expression told him she was not impressed with his choice of restaurants.

"You'll love the food here," he insisted. "Really."

Unconvinced, Claire followed him inside and

discovered that all her fears from looking at the outside were completely justified. It was a dive bar. But she was famished and the most divine smells were coming from the kitchen. It was a definite contradiction for sure.

They sat at a small table off to the side of the bar after Zeke greeted the bartender. She figured that he must be a regular because he called Zeke by his name. Claire took a tissue from her pocket and wiped off the chair before she sat down.

"Snob," he teased.

"No, I… ah…"

"It's fine," he grinned. "It's probably a good idea," he winked.

She blushed… again.

A harsh looking woman approached them with a pad and pen.

"Hey Jenny," Zeke smiled.

"Hi, hun," she replied. "What'll it be?"

"I'll take a lager. Claire? What would you like?"

"Uh, a white wine?"

Jenny chuckled and then broke into a smoker's cough. "I'll see if we have a bottle. We don't get a lot of requests here for white wine," she mocked.

"Well then," Claire stammered. "I'll take… um…"

"Same as me," Zeke finished for her. "If there's no wine, she'll have a lager."

"I don't like beer," she hissed.

"You haven't tried the right beer then."

"Are you eating?" Jenny interrupted.

"Yep. What do you want Claire?"

"There's no menu," she glared at him.

"I know. What do you want to eat?"

"How am I supposed to order?"

"We'll have two cheeseburgers, fries and let's start with mozz sticks."

Jenny left with their order and Claire sat with a blank look on her face.

Zeke snickered. "Have you never been to a place like this?"

"Never." She was horrified.

"I come here all the time. Best burgers this side of the Mississippi."

Claire didn't argue. It really did smell wonderful and her stomach was betraying her by growling loudly. Zeke laughed and they sipped on their beers, after they'd been delivered, and waited for their food.

*****

Brent was in disbelief. He'd had him beaten up. He'd personally threatened him with a lawsuit, yet Zeke had defied him and taken his girl to dinner, at a hole-in-the-wall piece of shit dive, no less. Claire was too good for places like that. He thought he'd made it perfectly clear that she was his, and no one else's, and he wanted her back where she belonged. He was livid. Oh, Zeke would pay. He would most definitely pay for this.

He walked across the street and stood next to Zeke's truck then took his key and left a message that could not be misinterpreted.

19.

"See?" he crowed. "You loved the burger, ate *all* your fries, *and* drank a beer."

"A first for me," she admitted with a hint of a smile.

Zeke threw two twenty dollar bills on the table and they both stood and walked to the door. Several of the 'regulars' had arrived while they were eating and the bar was mostly full. Claire was relieved they were leaving, though she'd never offend Zeke by telling him. It was kind of him to feed her and she would be as gracious as she could.

"Thank you for dinner," she added as they walked into the fading sun. "The food *was* good."

"That was hard for you, wasn't it?" he chuckled.

"What?" she feigned innocence.

"You had prejudged the place before we'd even stepped in the front door."

"Well, who wouldn't?"

Zeke just laughed as he led her to his truck, stopping several feet away and gasping in horror. "Shit!" Scratched into the paint on the driver's door were the words 'fucking cunt.' He felt her knees go weak and caught her just as she crumbled. He heard the sobs and felt the violent shaking and his heart broke over and over again. Brent was nowhere in sight as Zeke glanced back and forth trying to find him. He'd left before he could see her reaction. The thought puzzled Zeke. Brent was such a monumental coward.

"Let's get you in the truck and home," he soothed as he lifted Claire into the front seat. He reached for the seatbelt and buckled her in then raced around the other side, taking another look at Brent's graffiti and then jumped in and drove quickly home.

Claire was slumped over, her chin on her chest and quietly crying. If he could get away with it, Zeke would just kill the bastard, but he wasn't worth going to jail for. He pulled his truck into the driveway and carried her to the front door. He wrestled with his keys and shoved open the front door. Claire's arms were around his neck and her head rested on his shoulder. Zeke could feel his t-shirt dampening with her tears. As he bent over to place her on the couch, her arms tightened and the trembling began once more, so he just sat with Claire in his lap and held her while thinking of all the ways he wanted to physically torture the asshole who'd done this to the beautiful woman in his arms.

Eventually, Claire cried herself to sleep, still in the safety and warmth of Zeke's strong arms. He knew he should try to lay her on the sofa, but selfishly he continued to hold her, smelling her hair and feeling her warm breath on his neck. His whole life he'd been taught to stand up and defend the little guy… the underdog… the bullied. And he had many times. With Claire, however, the feelings were completely different. He didn't just want to defend her. He wanted to protect her… to care for her… to make her smile… to love her.

Yeah, he thought. *I want to love her.*

*****

Claire awoke but didn't open her eyes. She was so comfortable and warm that she relished the feeling and wanted to prolong it as long as possible. And then he moved. Her eyes flung open and she recognized who she was on… who was cradling her.

"I'm sorry," she muttered as she moved to sit up.

"You have nothing to be sorry for," he groaned as she wiggled in his lap, sending shivers of delight through his body.

"This *is* all my fault," she argued. "If it wasn't for me you wouldn't have been beaten up and your truck wouldn't need to be fixed. I'd say I have a lot to be sorry for."

"Listen to me very carefully," Zeke chided. "Nowhere is it written that you have to go through life all by yourself with no one to help you. I walked into this situation with my wide eyes open. And you forgot to add the lawsuit he's threatening me with," he teased.

"Yeah," she sighed.

"Hey!" He placed both his hands on her cheeks and lifted her face to him. "I'm teasing you. I don't give a shit about the truck. It's an easy fix. The bruises will heal and Brent has no reason to sue me. I have GPS proof that my truck did not hit his car on State Street like he claims. He can line up every attorney in the city and it won't matter. I'm not worried about it so don't let it worry you. Please?"

He saw the single tear fall and he wiped it away with his thumb leaving behind a glistening spot on her cheek. Without thinking he leaned in and kissed the moisture away. She stiffened.

"I'm sorry. I shouldn't have done that."

"No, it's just that…"

"Let's get you to bed," he changed the subject.

That's when Claire noticed they weren't in her apartment. "Where are we?"

"My house. It's safer for you here and I have a guest room with a real bed," he teased again.

"Oh. I don't want to be a bother."

"You aren't. Although if you keep arguing with me you might become one," he grinned. "Let me get you something to sleep in."

He left the living room giving her a chance to inspect her surroundings. It was nothing like she would've imagined, not that she'd imagined about his house. But if she had, this would not have been it.

It had a dark wood floor and pale blue walls and not a TV in sight. She'd pegged him for watching football on Sunday with a bottle of beer in his hand. On the walls were two magnificent abstract paintings that gave the room charm and interest. A large sectional sofa took up two walls. It was plush fabric in beige with several throw cushions in shades of blue and brown. A large wooden oval coffee table was in the middle of the room and two armless chairs sat in front of the window with a small table between them. It was tastefully decorated and didn't scream bachelor pad at all.

Zeke returned with a t-shirt and handed it to her. "Let me show you to your room."

Claire followed behind him. It wasn't a large house at all. There was a kitchen and small dining area and the hallway led to one small room that appeared to be Zeke's office, a bathroom and another bedroom with a bed and chair in it, where she would stay. Another door led off the hallway, presumably the master bedroom, but the door was closed.

"Bathroom is across the hall," he informed her. "I've put fresh towels in there and I'll be right across the hall in that room," pointing to the closed door, "if you need me… or anything," he stammered.

"I'll be fine, thank you."

"Okay then. Goodnight." He closed the door behind him.

After her nap she wasn't all that tired. She looked around at the room. Off-white carpet on the floor, walls painted a pale yellow, the bedhead and nightstand white, with a yellow plaid armchair in the corner. Another tastefully decorated room. Zeke Dayton was baffling her for sure.

Claire kicked off her shoes and was just about to change into the shirt Zeke had given her when she remembered she had homework. "Ugh," she sighed. Her backpack was still in the truck… she hoped. Very softly she opened the door and crept down the hall. Rounding the corner to the front door she came face to face with a hard, warm, bare chest. "Oh!" she mouthed.

"Are you sneaking out?" he growled.

"Um, no."

"Good."

There was something in his voice that had her heart pounding. She was just staring at the bare skin in front of her eyes, his hard nipples standing at attention.

"So where are you headed?" he asked softly.

"My… my backpack," she stuttered.

"On the chair," he answered with a nod. "Already got it for you."

"Thank you."

"You're welcome."

They continued to stand, Claire looking at Zeke's chest and Zeke inhaling the scent of her hair. Several seconds ticked by on the wall clock. Neither of them moving.

"Did you want me to carry it through for you?" he asked.

"What?" she moaned, her eyes now closed as she felt

the heat radiating from his body and the scent of his cologne filling her.

"Your backpack."

"Where?"

He chuckled. With great restraint he kissed her on the top of her head and stepped backwards leaving Claire to sigh in resignation that he was gone. He picked up her backpack and walked down the hall with Claire close on his heels. The backpack was dropped inside the door and Zeke stood aside so she could enter.

"Goodnight Claire," he whispered and once again closed the door behind her.

How long she stood staring at the closed door she didn't know. Conflicting emotions raged a war inside her. Men were scum. She wanted to be loved. Men couldn't be trusted. He smelled soooo good. Men were cruel. He'd been so kind. Men lied to get what they wanted. Zeke could have taken her right then and she wouldn't have stopped him. She never wanted to have sex again. How she'd wanted to lean in and bite his nipple.

Trying to clear her mind, she pulled her laptop and her books from her backpack, changed into the t-shirt, which smelled of *him*, and tried to prepare for midterms.

She awoke the next morning to the smell of bacon. Claire loved bacon!

*****

There was no point in trying anymore. Sleep wouldn't come no matter what he did so Zeke sat up in bed and clicked on the television hanging on the opposite wall. At least SportsCenter would keep him company. He wanted something else… *someone* else, and it was frustrating him. Telling himself over and over again that she wasn't his type wasn't helping.

After hearing the same stories on the program he was watching for the second time, Zeke gave up ever getting to sleep and got out of bed. It still hurt to put weight on his leg but he couldn't just lie there staring at the ceiling. He grabbed the jeans he'd been wearing just a few hours ago and pulled them up his thighs. He stood at Claire's door for a moment longer than necessary and then walked into the kitchen and pulled the jug of orange juice from the fridge. He unscrewed the lid and chugged, wiped his mouth with the back of his hand and put the jug back on the shelf. *Now what?* he wondered. There were always bills to pay so he meandered to his office, straightening a couple of pictures on the walls along the way and picking up a stray dust bunny on the floor. He settled into his office chair and tackled the thing he most hated – bookkeeping.

Before he knew it, two hours had passed. His checkbook was balanced, principal and interest paid on loans and credit cards entered into his accounting software, and his desk straightened and tidy. Now he was tired, but it was already after five so coffee would be next on the agenda.

After his third cup he decided to make breakfast. He rarely ate at home but managed to scrounge some bacon from the freezer, which he defrosted in the microwave, and a couple of eggs. He wasn't sure how old they were but they smelled fine when he cracked them into a bowl. He whisked them with some milk and put two slices of bread in the toaster. He was feeling quite proud of himself when he heard a door open.

20.

"You made breakfast," she grinned.

"I did. I hope you like bacon and eggs. I haven't got anything else."

"Bacon is my favorite food," she admitted with a big smile. "A man after my own heart."

That stopped Zeke dead in his tracks. He glanced up to look at the woman sitting at the counter wearing his t-shirt, her bare legs taunting him.

"Please tell me you like it crispy."

She was just talking about bacon. The comment about her heart meant nothing more than their shared love of bacon. Was he relieved?

"I do… almost crumbling crispy."

"Oh, me too!" she cried. "I hope you made a lot."

"The whole package."

"I can eat the package."

Zeke gulped. How could he take everything she was saying about bacon and turn it into something else? *I'm after her heart and she could eat my whole package*? he sighed. He was getting turned on just imagining.

"You okay?" she asked. "You have a pained expression on your face."

"I didn't get much sleep last night."

"You should go back to bed then."

Only if you're coming with me! "I have a busy day ahead. No rest for the wicked." He took the plates to the counter and then slid her eggs out of the pan and put a big pile of bacon in front of her. "My lady," he bowed.

"I could kiss you," she laughed as she took two pieces off the top of the stack. "I'm starving!"

"God," he groaned.

"Seriously, are you okay?"

"Yeah," he replied as he limped around to slide onto the stool next to her.

"Your leg is really bothering you, huh?"

"It'll be fine," he shrugged.

"I am so sorry," she began.

"Not again!" he warned. "I told you. You have *nothing* to be sorry for. He's the prick, not you."

"But…"

"Seriously Claire. I'll have to gag you if you don't stop apologizing," he teased.

"How about I just stick bacon in my mouth instead?"

"Good idea," he muttered and poured himself another cup of coffee.

They ate in silence, well, almost silence. Zeke thought Claire sounded like she was having an orgasm with each piece of bacon she ate. It drove him nuts as he watched her salivating and chewing each piece. Then she'd lick her fingers, one at a time and it was like he was watching porn in slow motion. He was thoroughly captivated by her. She appeared so innocent and child-like, yet he knew that her life experience had left her anything but innocent. Yet, here she sat, in an oversized shirt, hair in a bun on top of her head and devoid of all makeup and he'd never seen a more beautiful creature in his life. And that was another thing about her that he found attractive. She really had no idea just how beautiful she was. Even though she'd been used for the last several years as nothing more than an ornament to be paraded around, she didn't have that conceit and arrogance that so many women had.

"Thanks so much for breakfast," she said, interrupting his thoughts. "Time to get ready for school." She jumped off the stool and went to her room, leaving Zeke to sit and watch her go, her hips swinging as each naked leg took a step.

Within fifteen minutes she was back in the kitchen ready to get to class. "Can I help you with the dishes?"

"Nope," Zeke smiled. "In the dishwasher already."

"Well I timed that perfectly, didn't I," she giggled.

"You ready to go?"

"Yep."

He grabbed his keys and took Claire's backpack from her and walked to the front door.

"Are you gonna carry my books for me?"

He smiled. "Get in the truck."

As Claire stepped off the front porch she was harshly brought back to the reality of her life. In the daylight, Brent's artwork looked worse than the evening before. He'd sent his message loud and clear.

"What I don't understand," she whispered, more to herself than to Zeke, "is if he hates me so much, why does he want me back?"

"Because he needs to control something and you allowed him to control *you*."

Her head whipped up and she stared at him. "That was mean."

"It wasn't meant to be. I'm sorry."

"But it's true," she grimaced. "I allowed it all."

"No. Not all. Mom texted and wants you to stop by this evening. You should talk this out with her."

"I will," she said. "Are you going to be able to get that fixed?" she nodded at the truck door.

"Of course!" he shrugged. "I can do anything," he chuckled.

"I bet you can."

Zeke dropped her off at her apartment after making sure Brent was nowhere to be seen. Claire needed to grab a couple of things before her first class and then she'd drive over to Susan's after her last class. She waved goodbye to Zeke as she opened her front door and stepped inside. Her books were on her desk in her bedroom and once she had them she'd be on her way to her statistics class. But she didn't make it to her desk. She froze once she saw the roses lying on her bed. Red. Her favorite color.

There was a card resting on the red satin bow that tied the stems together. Her throat went dry and her palms were clammy. He'd been here... in her home. He'd gotten in. She wondered if she'd ever be free of him.

If it hadn't been mid-terms she wouldn't have gone to school. She would have headed straight to Susan's, but she'd let Brent derail her academic plans once before and she wasn't going to do it again. So she made it through her three exams, becoming angrier and angrier, and then walked home to get her car.

"How dare he?" she asked herself. "I am not his to do with as he pleases anymore." That sobered her instantly. Zeke had been right. She'd allowed Brent to do as he pleased. She'd handed him control without even realizing it. *What would have happened if I'd stood up to him... just once?* she thought. But she'd never know... or would she?

*****

"I need a driver!" Claire announced as she walked into the Dayton family home. "Who's in?"

Bill and Susan looked up when she walked into the family room. Bill was doing a crossword puzzle in the newspaper and Susan was reading a book.

"A driver for what?" Bill asked, without looking up.

"For a mission," Claire declared. "I need to tape a note on Brent's front door and I don't want to go alone."

"I'll go!" Bill and Susan said in unison.

"Okay," she skeptically replied. "You both want to come?"

"If you're going to Brent's we are both coming," Susan answered emphatically. "You think we'd let you go alone?"

"Right. I just need to find a piece of paper and decide what I want to say." Claire pulled a notebook from her backpack and a pen. She sat at the table and chewed on the end of her pen for about ten seconds and then began writing furiously for several minutes. Bill and Susan watched her, with glances to each other periodically. When Claire had finished she asked for some tape to take with them. Susan directed her to the junk drawer in the kitchen.

With paper and tape in hand, Claire said, "Well, let's go."

Bill and Susan scrambled to their feet and Bill announced that he was driving.

"I have no problem with that," Claire stated. "In fact, it will be like a getaway car," she winked.

Susan was thrilled to see Claire ready to confront

Brent, even if it was only in a letter. It was a start… a start to reclaiming her life… a start to putting the past where it belonged – behind her. And she would be there to support her in any way she needed.

The drive into the city took about twenty minutes and there was little conversation inside Bill's truck. He was concentrating on driving in the traffic, Susan was thinking how proud she was of Claire, and Claire was just trying to keep her teeth from chattering. It had seemed a brilliant idea at the time, but as they drove closer her nerves were getting the best of her. However, she was determined.

Claire navigated their way to the street where she used to live… to the rows of townhouses where the rich lived… to the house that she'd thought would make all of her dreams come true. How naïve she'd been. Bill found a parking spot across the street and put the truck in park.

"Well," he stated the obvious. "We're here."

"We are," Claire nodded. In her hands was the piece of paper she'd written her message to Brent on and on the dash sat the roll of tape.

"Do you want me come with you?" Susan asked.

"No." Claire shook her head and took a deep breath. "This is something I need to do on my own."

"Good for you," Bill encouraged. "We'll be right here."

"Thanks," Claire smiled and opened the door. She checked for traffic and then crossed the street. The odds of Brent being home were slim, nevertheless, she wanted to be speedy – no dawdling. She ran up the front steps to the front door, opened the wrought iron screen door and ripped a piece tape off and stuck it to the paper and then stuck it to the door. The paper was folded in half with his name scrawled on the back. She'd memorized the words she'd written… words that had come straight from her heart.

Brent –

You had your chance and you screwed it up. You hurt me – badly, and for that I will never forgive you. I gave my life and my heart to you and you pounded it to a pulp. There is no chance I would ever consider coming back to you. EVER! Stop stalking me. Stop coming to my apartment or I will get a restraining order. And do not hurt the people that have been so kind to me. Zeke Dayton is not my boyfriend. He is my boss. Leave him out of it. If you have something to say to me, then say it to ME!

I hope that you can deal with your issues so that at some point you can have a healthy relationship but it will never be with me. That ship has sailed.

Goodbye,

Claire

"I did it!" she bawled as she jumped back into the truck. "I did it."

Susan cradled her in her arms as Claire wept into her breast. Bill pulled the truck into traffic and drove away, back to the suburbs… back home.

21.

"I let him do it, didn't I? I just handed him control of my life."

"Oh Claire, honey," Susan soothed as she put the coffee pot on the hot pad in the middle of the table. "He took it from you, but you didn't stop him. And it's not nearly as black and white as you think."

"But I didn't fight him, physically or emotionally."

"Physically fighting him would have left you dead. That would not have been a smart idea in my opinion," Susan replied with soberness. "It's a complicated relationship and I am certainly not a psychiatrist but I do know a couple of things. You took a huge step in taking control when you ran from him. That took courage to walk away with nothing. I think you knew deep down that he would probably kill you one day. Each time he physically hurt you it escalated, right?"

Claire nodded as she remembered the horrific events.

"The escalation would have continued until one day..." Susan didn't finish the sentence.

"I think that after... after he... raped me, I knew that he thought he could do anything he wanted and I would just take it. I could never have gone through that again. I guess that's why Greta killed herself."

"Who's Greta?" asked Susan.

"The woman I almost became," whispered Claire, horrified that their lives seemingly paralleled, and taking solace in the fact that she'd been strong enough to walk away. "I wonder if she'd ever tried to leave?" she said to herself.

"If the man is powerful it's very difficult to break away, especially if he doesn't want her to leave."

"I guess that's why she escaped the only way she could. To think that killing herself was her only way out, that's just heartbreaking."

"It is," agreed Susan. "Thank God you didn't get to that point," she said and took Claire's hand in hers. "What you did today told him you were taking back the control. That's a good thing."

"Will it make him mad?" Claire feared.

"I don't know. Maybe you should stay here just to be on the safe side."

"She's staying with me," Zeke commanded as he walked into the kitchen. "She'll be safe at my house. He won't get to her even if he tries."

Susan looked up at her son and saw the fierceness and protectiveness in his eyes and his tight lips. It startled her for a brief moment until…

"I think that's a wonderful idea. I agree wholeheartedly," she smiled.

"I really don't think that's necessary," Claire countered.

"I do. He's an asshole. Oh, sorry Mom," Zeke grimaced.

"He is," Susan agreed. "Humor an old woman, would you?"

"You are *not* old," scoffed Claire.

"Older than you," she laughed. "I think until we know he's completely out of the picture it would be a good idea to have a big strong man to protect you. And, he's not bad to look at either."

"Thanks, mom," Zeke smirked.

And he wasn't bad to look at. The stereotypical tall dark and handsome described Zeke perfectly.

"Fine! But I'd like to have my car so I can go to school on my own like a big girl," she pleaded. "And I'd like to stop at my apartment and get some things."

"We can do that." Zeke accepted her conditions.

"Would you like to stay for dinner?" Susan asked.

"Nope, but thanks," Zeke answered quickly. "I am going to take Claire to a place that won't creep her out like last night's restaurant," he grinned.

"I told you the food was good!" Claire exclaimed.

"I know. But tonight I'll take you to another one of my favorites. It's a little more, shall we say, *uptown*."

"Are you saying I'm a snob?" Claire asked indignantly.

"If the shoe fits."

"Argh!" She grabbed for her shoe and yanked it off her foot. "I think it does!" she laughed as she hurled it at him, smacking him on the arm.

Susan watched the exchange with a smile forming on her lips.

*****

"I know exactly what you're thinking," Zeke smirked as he sat across the booth from Claire.

"You cannot know what I'm thinking!"

"I can," he affirmed. "But I really want to hear you say it anyway."

"Say what?"

"Say it. I know you're thinking it so just say it."

Claire squirmed in her seat. "I think the food last night was better," she mumbled, looking down at her napkin in her lap.

"What's that? I didn't quite catch what you were saying."

Claire repeated herself, mumbling even more.

"Is it really that hard to admit?"

"The food last night was better!" she all but shouted. "There. Happy?"

"Very," Zeke chuckled.

"But this is good," Claire added as she took another bite of her lasagna.

"You need a couple of good helpings of pasta," Zeke noted. "Put some meat on those bones."

"My bones don't need meat," she declared.

"Do you even weigh one hundred pounds?" he asked

"Yes."

"Barely," he added.

"Thin is in."

"Thin is fine. Skinny is unhealthy." He was serious and his expression showed it.

"Says a man!"

"A man who doesn't like scrawny and unhealthy women." It slipped out before he had a chance to check himself and leave that statement unsaid.

"What type of women do you usually date?" Claire asked.

It appeared that she hadn't understood the intent from his last sentence, or she was ignoring it. Whichever it was, he was relieved.

"I haven't dated in a while."

"How long is a while?"

"Um. Fifteen months?"

"Wow. A hot single guy like you? I thought you'd be out with a different girl every week."

He looked up at her. She was looking at him. Their eyes locked. And then Claire cleared her throat and broke the spell as she took another bite.

"Nah," he shook his head. "There hasn't been anyone in a while."

"But there was someone?"

"Nobody that matters now." His heart wanted him to keep talking… to tell her he'd developed deep feelings for her. But his head told him to keep his mouth shut. He listened to his head.

"That's too bad," she eventually said. "I'm sure you'd make a lucky girl very happy."

"I hope to."

*****

With a bag full of clothes, Claire pulled into Zeke's driveway, with him right behind her. He'd taken her back to her car after dinner, they'd driven to her apartment where he waited in the living room while she collected her things, and then he followed her back to his house in his truck. If he had anything to say about it she wouldn't ever be leaving, but he knew that was not only presumptuous, but also premature. Claire had to become her own woman before she'd be ready to be in a relationship.

"Coffee?" he asked.

"I really have to study," she sighed. "I have two more midterms tomorrow."

"I'll have breakfast ready at seven," he smiled. "Gotta send you off with a full stomach."

"Thanks, Dad. That's really sweet of you."

He sort of blushed and it made her giggle.

"What?" he asked.

"You're blushing."

"I am not! Men don't blush."

"This one does," she said as she slapped him on his stomach.

"Ah," he winced ever so slightly.

"Still sore? I'm sorry."

"It'll be fine."

"Yeah. You're a big tough guy, huh?"

"You have no idea," he whispered.

She looked up at him with those big innocent green eyes and he was wholly overcome with love for the woman in front of him. Yes, she was indeed scrawny. And yes, she was like a wounded bird, not quite ready to fly. And yes, she'd been in a destructive and abusive relationship, but that didn't negate all the amazing things he loved about her.

He pushed a lock of golden hair behind her ear, revealing her flawless porcelain skin. Yes, she was beautiful and turned the heads of all the men that saw her. But she was beautiful on the inside as well. She was kind and caring, smart and funny, and sexy as hell and at that moment all he wanted was to taste her lips.

"I'm sorry," he whispered as he leaned in closer.

"For what?"

"For this," he breathed on her lips. And then he touched his lips to hers and time stopped. For half a second Claire became as stiff as a board and then she softened and melted into his arms. He wrapped himself around her and held her to him as his lips explored hers. Catching himself, he pulled back before he ravaged her. He just held her close, her head on his chest, his hands running through her hair. The moment was perfect.

"Thank you," she murmured into his chest.

"For what?" It was his turn to ask.

"For reminding me I'm still alive, I'm still a woman and I deserve to be loved."

"You're welcome." A big smile spread across his face. "Now go study."

"Yes, sir."

He released her and she disappeared into her room leaving Zeke needing a cold shower.

22.

Three months had gone by since that fateful day when Claire had altered her future forever. She still couldn't believe that she'd run, especially in those heels! But she had and it had been the best decision of her life. In those three months she had pondered on her relationship with Brent and why she'd given away her soul to have nice things. *Things.* At the time she was sure Brent loved her and meant all of the promises he'd made, but now, three months away from him, she could see how it'd all been a lie. He'd said what he'd needed to say in order to get her to do what he needed her to do. He'd manipulated her and lied to her repeatedly and her eyes were finally wide open.

Staying with Zeke and becoming part of the Dayton family had also opened her eyes. Watching Bill and Susan together had buoyed her hope that true love really did exist and her faith in a happily ever after was being restored. On Sunday, as the whole family sat around the table and ate dinner together, Claire watched Rebekah and Rachel with their husbands, both doting on their wives… both respectful and kind. The truth that not all men are pigs was being reinforced every time she saw them together.

And then there was Zeke. It had been two weeks since he'd kissed her. It had been the most perfect kiss recorded in history. His lips were soft and warm and they'd danced with hers for a brief, sweet moment, long enough for her to enjoy and short enough that she hadn't felt threatened. When she'd awoken the next morning she'd wondered if there would be an awkwardness between them, but she'd been worried over nothing. Zeke was his usual charming self and she'd begun to look at him differently. She began looking beneath the surface and she liked what she saw.

She often thought about that kiss and all it meant to her. She'd thought of herself as a flower bud, having been closed for a season and now, with the bright sun shining down and warming her soul, her petals were opening for the first time… a rebirth of sorts… a new spring. She was seizing control of her destiny and the feeling was marvelous.

Midterms were over and she'd performed extremely well. Claire loved learning and loved reading, the combination making her a very good student. She was already considering what to do for employment after she'd graduated, even though she still had one more semester to go. Helping Zeke and Gearheads had reinforced her desire to work in the marketing field. She loved helping him and seeing the fruits of her hard work when Zeke would come home and tell her another new client found him on Facebook. It was exhilarating to say the least.

One evening after one such conversation while cleaning up the dinner dishes, Claire broached the subject of paying for her car. She still had money left and wanted to take care of her obligation.

"I need to pay you something," she insisted.

"And I've told you that you don't."

"But you shouldn't be out money because I needed a car."

"This week alone I've had three new clients come to the garage for work done. They all came from Yelp. I didn't set up a Yelp page. I don't even know what Yelp is!" He stared at her waiting for an answer.

"Yelp is an online directory. It helps people find local businesses, and…"

"And you set it up for me." It was more a statement than a question.

"I did."

"Those three jobs will *more* than cover the cost of your car. And that's only this week. I'm not out money because of you, Claire. I'm *making* money because of you."

"But..."

"Dammit, Claire!" he yelled.

Her reaction was instant. She physically shrunk into the corner and she looked like a frightened animal. He knew what he'd done the second the words left his lips.

"Oh, Claire," he pleaded. "I'm so sorry. Please forgive me." He hurried to her and encircled her in his arms. She was rigid for several seconds causing him to worry that he'd permanently damaged their relationship. The last thing she needed was a man screaming at her. And then, she softened. He heard her held breath exhale and she relaxed in his arms. His worst fear was alleviated, but then, he felt the slight whimper as her body shuddered.

"Don't cry," he whispered. "Please don't cry." He stroked her hair and rubbed her back and felt her pain and desperately wanted to take it from her. In that moment their physical and emotional connection was permanently fused and he knew without a doubt that she was his destiny. For as long as he lived his purpose in life would be to protect her from harm and love her unconditionally, and as long as she was with him, in whatever capacity she chose, he would be a content man.

"I would never hurt you. You know that, right?" he asked softly.

She nodded and sniffed.

"I want you to know that as far as I'm concerned, the

car is paid for in full. Okay?"

She nodded and sniffed again.

"In fact, I owe you money." That got a response.

"No!" Her head whipped up and she looked at him. "No you don't!"

"The number of new customers I've had over the past several weeks has been overwhelming. I never believed your ideas would work as well as they have."

"Thanks," she muttered with a frown.

He laughed. "I should be paying you for the time you've put into it."

"No! You gave me a car! You don't owe me anything,"

"Exactly my point!" he laughed. "That's how *I* feel. You owe me *nothing*!"

"Okay," she finally agreed.

"Seriously? I've actually convinced you?" he laughed.

"Yes. You've actually convinced me," she sighed.

"You won't bring it up again?" He was pushing it.

"No," she said, a hint of a smile showing.

"Hallelujah!" he cheered.

That got a full-blown chuckle from her and he'd never been so pleased with himself.

"Wanna try and beat me at Super Mario Brothers?" he winked.

"You mean, do you wanna try and beat *me*?" she teased.

"You're on."

They ran down the hall and into Zeke's bedroom.

Claire jumped on the bed and scooted to the end and crossed her legs. She took the controller he handed her and straightened her back.

"You're gonna lose," she grinned.

He loved it when she trash talked, especially because in the several games they'd played he'd won every time.

"You're pretty cocky there," he chuckled. "Wanna place a bet on it?"

Her grin disappeared. "Like what?" she questioned.

"Oh, I don't know," he lied. He knew exactly what he wanted. "The winner gets to pick the next game we play?"

"Deal."

Oh, I think I'm going to like this, he thought.

*****

It had been two weeks since Brent had found the note from Claire taped to his front door. It had been two weeks of revisiting his plan on how to get her back. Philip's way hadn't worked. Brent had done everything Philip had told him to do… everything that had worked on his women. When Brent finally accepted that it wasn't working, he also noted that Philip was twice divorced and his third wife had committed suicide. Should this really be the man he was taking relationship advice from? He was going to have to come up with Plan B. What that was, however, he had no idea.

23.

"I don't know why you're pouting," Zeke laughed. "You haven't won a single game against me. You should be used to losing by now."

"Well, you'd think I was due one then wouldn't you?" she pouted.

"Claire, just accept that I am the master at Super Mario and that you'll never beat me," he mocked with bravado.

Folding her arms, she made a "HMPH" and continued pouting.

"Are you ready to play my game now?"

"Fine. What is it?"

"Spin the bottle," he grinned.

"What? Are you serious?"

"Deadly."

"Do we even have a bottle?"

"Do we even have a bottle?" Zeke mocked again. "I'm a guy who likes beer," he chuckled. "I have a bottle."

"Oh," she frowned. There was no way she was getting out of it.

"I'll go get one," and he disappeared from the bedroom.

Claire continued to sit on the king-sized bed, but her legs were cramping from sitting so long. She straightened them and leaned back, her head on the plush comforter. It was a comfortable bed, the mattress molding to her spine and curves. She closed her eyes and pretended she was floating on a cloud.

"Hey sleeping beauty," he said. "Don't pretend to be tired to get out of playing."

"I'm not," she sighed wistfully. "I'm just enjoying your mattress."

"Is your bed not comfortable?" he worried.

"Oh, it's fine," she replied. "Yours is just better."

"It should be," he quipped. "I paid thousands of dollars for it."

"Money does buy happiness," she said.

"No, it doesn't," he countered.

Claire opened her eyes and sat up. She looked right at him and said, "No. You're right. It doesn't."

He could have taken her in his arms right then and kissed her senseless. Instead, he produced the empty bottle from behind his back and said, "Ready?"

"Ready as I'll ever be," she muttered.

"Floor!" he commanded.

She slid to the floor and sat opposite him, once again cross-legged.

"The rules," he began. "Three choices: Truth, Dare, or Clothes."

"Clothes?" she gasped. "I know truth and dare, but what's clothes?"

"You remove one article of clothing," he winked.

"Oh, no!"

"Oh, yes! You agreed that the winner got to pick the game. I'm the winner and this is *my* game. Are you going back on your word?"

She thought about it for a brief second and then

pouted. "Fine."

"Good," he grinned. "Ladies first." He handed her the bottle.

Hesitantly, she took it from him and laid it on the carpet in between them and then, with a deep breath, she spun it. It circled around and around and landed in between them, more towards Zeke. She breathed a sigh of relief.

"Truth," he said.

"Oh no! I get to choose which one you're doing."

"If that makes you happy," he shrugged. "Fine."

"Okay. Truth. First kiss?"

"I was seven," he began.

"Of course you were," she laughed.

"We were in first grade and it was under the slide. Raylene Everhart. But she kissed me!" He grabbed the bottle and spun it, landing on him again.

"Clothes," she mumbled.

"Really?" He was shocked.

"Take off your shirt."

"Yes, ma'am."

Claire told herself not to react once his shirt was off but it was tremendously difficult once she saw his abs. Defined and chiseled, she desperately wanted to reach out and trace the outline with her finger, but she refrained. Maybe it wasn't such a good idea for him to be shirtless. Claire found it difficult to look anywhere else.

"Spin," he said.

So she did and it landed smack dab on her.

"Ah," he grinned mischievously. "Truth. Your first kiss."

She didn't want to answer that and her face expressed her dislike of the question.

"I told you mine," he encouraged but she still didn't speak. "Come on Claire."

"Brent," she whispered. "It was Brent."

"A little older than seven," he said, trying to lighten the mood.

"Just a little," she agreed.

"My turn," and he spun the bottle, once again landing on Claire. "Clothes," he said. "Fair is fair," he winked at her.

Claire looked down at her attire. She was in panties and shorts, a bra and a t-shirt. Her feet were bare. "Damn! Of all the days not to keep my shoes on." She unzipped her shorts and wriggled out of them, folding them neatly beside her.

Zeke's gaze travelled from the tips of her toes, up her calves, over her knees and up her thighs 'til he caught sight of her leopard print panties. His eyes were drawn to them and unconsciously he licked his lips, Claire catching the response and sending a shiver up her spine. His scrutiny of her lower half was a tad unnerving, but there was a look in his eyes that didn't scare her. Rather, it made her feel desired and sexy… and she liked it.

"Your turn," Zeke purred.

She spun and it landed on her again. "Damn."

"Clothes."

She looked him squarely in the eye and reached for the hem of her shirt and pulled it over her head, the only time breaking eye contact when her shirt covered her face.

"Holy smokes!" Zeke uttered. "You are a goddess worthy of eternal worship." He couldn't peel his eyes away.

"Well, thank you, I guess."

"No. Thank *you*. You are truly the perfect female form. Although, you do need a little more meat on those bones," he added with a smile.

"More lasagna maybe?" she quipped.

"Maybe," he smiled.

For weeks they'd lived under the same roof and acted like roommates, with the exception of that one simply perfect kiss. They got along famously with similar senses of humor and taste in movies and television shows. Several evenings had been spent lying on his bed watching episodes of Game of Thrones and the Showtime comedy Episodes. They both loved Matt LeBlanc and were excited when they found a rerun of Friends on a cable channel. They ate Chinese take-out from a box and then said goodnight and retired to their separate bedrooms for the night, only to do it all over the next day. They liked each other as human beings and respected the other's work ethic and morals. They were perfect for each other but the thought scared Claire to death. How could she ever trust a man again after all that she'd been through? How could she ever think to give herself completely to a man after her experience with Brent? How could she love fully without always wondering when he would betray her?

Zeke was so different from Brent though - night and day different. He was laid back and easy-going and nothing really riled him. The only time she'd seen him frustrated was with her over the payment of the car… and that conversation had ended sublimely. Zeke was kind and sensitive to other's feelings. He was confident yet not arrogant. He was firm but not harsh. He was funny but not cruel. He was all the things Brent wasn't. Yet, her financial future always weighed heavily on her mind. With Brent she never had to worry about money - Never! And that was what she was sure she wanted out of life. Financial security. Was there more that she'd been missing?

Her mind was a whirlwind of thought as she and Zeke stared at each other, their eyes not even blinking. Her stomach was in knots as she battled within herself.

"You don't have to make any life decisions right now," he whispered. "I can see you are thinking about something and I want you to clear your mind of everything except this moment… right here in this room… right now with me."

She blinked. Could she do that? Could she put everything aside and let him do whatever he was thinking? Could she not be the Claire she'd always been, just for a little while?

Zeke crawled up onto his knees and leaned over so he was a mere inch from her face. "Don't think," he purred. "Just feel." And he kissed her.

His lips were like a cloud - soft and warm and the shiver started on the back of her neck and stretched all the way down to her toes. She lifted her head to him, returning the kiss and opening her mouth just a little as he deepened the kiss and tasted her lips with the tip of his tongue. She did feel. She felt him and he felt exquisite. As his tongue entered her mouth she felt it all. She felt the desire build deep in her body as his tongue danced a sweet and soft dance with hers. There was no aggression. There was no urgency. It was soft and silky and ever so nice. When he pulled away she was sorry the kiss had ended.

"How did that feel?" he asked.

"Nice," she smiled.

"Nice? I can do better than nice." And he kissed her again.

Her hands, planted firmly on the ground beside her, reached for his arms and rested on his biceps. They flinched and hardened under her touch. She squeezed as he once again pushed his tongue deep into her mouth and tasted her, reveling in the warmness of her, and her eager response.

When their breathing became shallow and ragged, he pulled back once more. "I want to go further but I don't want to scare you," he admitted.

"I don't feel scared," she marveled. "Not one bit."

Zeke climbed to his feet and reached down for her. She placed her hands in his and he pulled her up to stand in front of him.

"You will tell me if anything I do scares you? Or makes you feel uncomfortable in any way? Just say the word and I'll stop. Okay?"

Claire meekly nodded and bit her lip. The gentleness of his voice and the delicate caress of his hands had touched her heart and her soul and she knew that she would never be scared in his arms. He scooped her into his arms like she weighed nothing more than a feather and he placed her on his bed. As she lay atop the comforter he gazed upon her with love and desire and the look in his eyes formed a lump in her throat and tears filled her eyes. No one had ever looked at her like that and in that moment she knew without a doubt that there was so much more to being happy than a new pair of shoes or a fancy house. As her heart beat strongly and her pulse quickened she knew that unconditional love was what had been missing from her life and the idea that she had found that looking into the eyes of this sweet man standing over her sent the tears spilling over and falling to the pillow below her head.

"Don't cry," he pleaded as he fell to his knees beside the bed. "I'll stop."

"No," she shook her head. "I don't want you to stop. I want you to look at me like that forever."

"I can do that," he promised with a smile. "I can love you forever."

24.

"You love me?" she asked incredulously.

"Of course I do," he grinned. "And have done for a while."

"But…"

"You weren't ready to see it or hear it," he shrugged. "But you asked so I told you and I don't regret one word. I do love you, Claire."

She smiled and wiped away the tears.

"You don't have to say anything. There's no pressure." He took her hand in his and brought it to his lips.

"I want to," she began. "I'm not sure I even know what love is anymore."

"Yes, you do," Zeke affirmed. "I see it in your eyes. You love me." He grinned a cheeky grin and Claire laughed.

"I do, do I?"

"Yes, you do."

"I do," she whispered. "At least I think I do."

"My leg hurts," Zeke frowned. "Move over."

Claire scooted over and Zeke climbed in beside her, his arm under her neck and snaked around and down to rest his hand on her hip, her head on his chest.

"Where you belong," he smiled. "You fit perfectly."

She snuggled closer into his body and closed her eyes as she listened to his heart beating, the steady rhythmic thumping soothing and melodic. With his left hand he played with the golden strands of her hair. Together they lay there for several minutes as they accepted and absorbed each other's declarations, Zeke with a silly grin on his face and Claire, her mind in a whirl at not only hearing, but seeing his love shine through his eyes bright and clear.

"Are you okay?" he finally asked.

She smiled and nodded. "I am. Very much okay."

"Would you stay here with me tonight?"

She nodded once more and Zeke struggled with the comforter to get it *over* them rather than under. Once settled, he clicked off the light switch beside his bed and they slept, wrapped tightly in one another's arms.

*****

The morning sun woke Claire first. She was still in the same spot - head on his chest and her hand splayed on his abdomen. He was still in his jeans and still asleep. Claire ran her finger over and over his torso, feeling his smooth warm skin and the hardness of his muscles just underneath. She smiled at his tousled dark brown hair and the sexy whiskers that covered his chin.

All night she'd dreamed of Zeke. Some dreams were sweet and beautiful as they made love under the stars on a brilliantly clear night, or held their newborn baby together. And some were horrific as she relived moments of her life with Brent as Zeke tried desperately to save her and couldn't. Now, as she lay beside him she had to remind herself that those miserable and uncertain days with Brent were in the past and she had a wonderful future to look forward to… a future with Zeke.

Her fingers continued to circle across his flesh and she felt his arms around her tighten.

"Better be careful," he growled.

"Mornin'" she grinned.

"Good morning. How'd you sleep?"

"Good. You?"

"Best night's sleep I've had in months."

"I'm glad."

"It's Saturday. What would you like to do today? I can play hooky from the garage."

"Mmm? How about we stay here?"

"That can be arranged," he chuckled and flipped her onto her back as he towered over her. He lowered himself onto her body and rested on his elbows, his hands cupping her face. "You are so beautiful, Claire." He kissed her… a light feathery kiss that stole her breath. And then he deepened the kiss and expressed how much he wanted her. She responded by hugging him firmly as she held him to her lips. "Let me love you," he whispered into her mouth. Her reply was to hold him tighter, granting him the permission he sought.

His hands moved from her face and slid down her sides until they cupped her ass and held her to him, the button on his jeans pressing into her. He felt her stiffen as she breathed in.

"I promise you that my hands will never touch your body unless they are giving you pleasure. I could never hurt you... I'd rather die than cause you pain. Do you believe me?"

Claire nodded and exhaled slowly.

"Only pleasure," he purred. "Only ever pleasure." He rolled them both over so that she was straddling him and his hands kneading and caressing her ass as his hands slid inside her silky panties. "Only pleasure," he repeated into her mouth as she kissed him again.

She felt his hardness pressing into her belly and gazed into his hooded eyes. He smiled at her, his perfectly straight white teeth dazzling her as she leaned over him. "I do love you, Zeke. I am coming to understand that I haven't known what love was until I fell in love with you… and your family. Thank you for teaching me."

"Let me show you," he said as his hands caressed her back until they came upon her bra. He flicked the two hooks open and pulled the straps from her shoulders, revealing, in all their glory, her perfectly round snow white breasts with two rosebud-like nipples just begging to be tasted. "May I?" he asked.

He saw the hesitation. It was brief and she tried to hide it, but he saw it. He knew what had happened to her but didn't know any of the horrid details… and didn't want to know. But he did know that if he was to truly win her, she would have to trust him implicitly, and for her to do that, he'd have to go slow… very slow, and prove to her that he was worthy of that trust.

"I don't understand what you've been through and it makes me sick that you've suffered so much. But I can help you heal. I can mend your broken heart. Let me love you 'til you forget the past... 'til all you remember is me."

"I want you Zeke. I do. I just need… I need…"

"All you have to say is stop and I will. Of that you have my word. I won't ever hurt you, Claire. Love isn't about hurting, it's about trusting. Will you trust me?"

She nodded and Zeke, without hesitation, lifted his head and sucked one hard bud into his mouth. His tongue rolled over it and his teeth nipped and tugged and Claire dropped her head as she moaned in pleasure. Taking the other nipple into his mouth, she felt the wetness in between her legs and the acute need of satisfaction drove her to roll her hips in a circular motion, grinding into his hardness.

"Should I stop?" he panted, desperately hoping her answer would be no.

"No," she gasped. "Don't stop. Don't ever stop."

"You're making me crazy," he growled. She just smiled and continued to feel pleasure with each movement until Zeke couldn't take anymore. He flipped her back over so she was once again on her back and kneeled in between her legs. He undid the button on his jeans and then lowered the zipper as she watched intently. Then he scrambled off the bed and shoved his jeans down his legs until he was able to step out of them. As he stood before her in his briefs, their eyes caught and he smiled then removed his briefs and stood before her stark naked.

"You are a god worthy of eternal worship," she whispered.

"Are you mocking me?" he grinned.

"Quite the opposite," she replied seriously. "You are a beautiful man, Zeke."

"Thank you," he blushed and she smiled. Climbing back onto the bed, he reached for her panties and drew them slowly down her legs and discarded them on the floor. He leaned over and kissed her belly button and then each of her hips and Claire's hands automatically went to his head where she ran her fingers through his hair as he left a trail of feathery kisses across her taut tummy and lower to the curly mound that captured his attention. He kissed lower and lower until he'd spread her legs wide and opened her up to him for the taking.

As his tongue touched that place that was begging for him, her body went rigid and her back arched as she pulled on his hair. The pleasure was almost too much to bear as she writhed underneath him, looking for climax. A profound moment for her as she gave herself to him in the most vulnerable and private way, Claire released herself from her past. She forgave herself for taking the blame for the actions of others and she gave herself permission to be happy. She accepted that without the experiences of her past she would never have been able to see, or feel, this very moment for what it truly was. It was beautiful and perfect and she would forever be bound to Zeke as the man who had captured her heart without her even knowing.

With each lick of his tongue, with each nip of his teeth, he brought her closer and closer to the powerful moment of explosion and satisfaction. As her body trembled and shook as her orgasm coursed through her, her fate was sealed.

Still gasping for breath, still experiencing quivers as she rejoiced in his skill, Zeke kissed his way up her body until he found her mouth. He kissed her with urgency and passion and she tasted her nectar on his tongue as he pressed it against hers. And then, he pushed his length into her and stilled as she accepted him with her body and with her heart once again.

"Home," he whispered. "In your arms and inside you will always be home from now on. Promise me you'll be my home."

"I promise," she smiled.

And with that guarantee Zeke withdrew himself and plunged back into her, making her moan with pleasure as he repeated the act over and over. Sweat dripped from them as their bodies united and brought them to the peak of ecstasy and as they tumbled over the edge they clung to one another until they eventually fell asleep, fulfillment and love filling them completely.

25.

"I thought you said you trusted me," Zeke reminded her. Claire looked at him with big eyes and she looked so fragile he almost gave in. *Almost*. "Either you trust me or you don't."

"I do, but…"

"No buts. If you trust me, put it on."

Claire took the helmet from him and studied it closely while she stalled a little longer. He was pushing the limits of her trust.

"The day is perfect for a ride. Blue sky and not a chance of rain. It's warm and no wind. I couldn't have requested anything better. Now please?" he pleaded.

"Okay," she sighed. She pulled the bike helmet onto her head and tightened the strap under her chin. Then she climbed onto the bike behind him and grabbed him around the waist.

"Hold on tight."

"Oh, I will," she muttered as he started the engine. The noise filled her ears and she clung to him even tighter if that was possible.

He took it slow, just staying in the neighborhood and not going above forty miles an hour. By the time they pulled into the Waffle House parking lot, he knew she was ready to be done… for a while. She slid off the bike first and Zeke followed. They both removed their helmets and placed them on the seat of his bike.

"I'm proud of you," he grinned from ear to ear. "You tried something new."

"It seems to be the weekend for that," she replied trying not to smile.

"And?" he continued. "Was it *so* bad?"

"I guess not," she shrugged.

"Let's go eat," he said as he grabbed her hand and led her to the front door of the restaurant. "I worked up quite an appetite this morning."

Once they were seated and had placed their order, they sat and held hands across the table, Zeke unable to peel his eyes from the golden haired beauty sitting opposite him. That morning after they'd made love, he'd taken her into his shower and had washed her and shampooed her hair and made love to her again as he held her against the tiled wall, the water and soap lather supplying ample lubrication as their bodies joined together. The image of her writhing against him as her excitement built, her legs wrapped around his hips, her hands gripping his shoulders like vices, her mouth open, her eyes closed and moaning in unrestrained passion was all he could see when he closed his eyes. He got an erection every time he blinked.

But even more amazing than the shower was the fact Claire got on his motorcycle with him. He'd asked her a number of times if she'd wanted to go for a ride and every time she declined hastily. He'd seen the trepidation in her eyes as he'd handed her the helmet but she trusted him enough to do as he'd asked. It meant the world to him, more than she could ever imagine.

"If I confess something to you will you promise to be kind?"

That question scared him. He'd been in love with her for weeks and after the past twenty-four hours he was head over heels a goner. Having held her in his arms all night and watching her as he'd made love to her had sealed the deal. He was hers to do with as she pleased. And now she had a confession? He took a deep breath and nodded, terrified of what she was about to say.

"I actually really enjoyed the ride. It's an exhilarating feeling."

"That's your confession?"

"Yep," she gulped.

He tossed his head back and laughed a loud bellowing laugh. "You had me so scared for a minute."

"Why?" His reaction surprised her.

"A confession? Would I be kind? I've just had the best night, and morning, of my life? I had no idea what you were gonna say."

"Oh," she grinned.

"I'm thrilled you love riding. There are so many beautiful places we can go."

"Well, I didn't say I *loved* it," she replied cheekily.

If it was possible, Zeke fell just a little more in love with her. Trying something new was definitely out of her comfort zone and he'd already pushed her to the max. She'd squeezed him so tight at times during their ride that he'd wondered if his diaphragm would survive the journey, but she'd done it. And now she was openly admitting that it had been a positive experience for her. She was defying all expectations he had and he was loving it.

The waiter arrived with their brunch and they dug in quickly, each needing to recharge after their *active* morning.

"If I eat any more," she moaned as she placed her knife and fork on her plate, "You'll be complaining I have too much meat on my bones."

"Never!"

"What if I get fat?"

"So what?" he frowned.

"Would you still love me? If I was morbidly obese?"

"Of course! What brought this on?" But he thought he knew already. The asshole Brent.

"Just curious," she shrugged.

"Don't compare me with that bastard. I'm nothing like him," he assured.

"I know that."

"Do you?"

She studied his face; his kind brown eyes, the smile wrinkles around them and his long dark lashes. She nodded.

"You don't have to be stick thin, or dressed in designer fashions, or drive the *right* car. I love what's on the outside, sure," he grinned and wiggled his eyebrows which made her giggle. "But I love even more who you are inside, Claire. That's much more important than the physical."

"I do love you." And she meant it.

Once they were finished and the bill paid, they headed out to the bike and the ride home.

"Do you mind if we make a quick stop at the garage?" he asked.

"Of course not," she smiled as she lifted her helmet from the seat.

"We won't be there long, I promise," he grinned and

kissed her before she put her helmet on. "And then we can go home."

"I'd like that," she smiled.

*****

She didn't cling to him as tightly as they left the parking lot and merged into traffic and as they pulled into Gearheads Claire told him that she was a little disappointed at how short the ride was. He promised to take the long way home.

The joy they were feeling quickly evaporated when they both turned and saw the black Land Rover in the parking space next to the garage. Zeke reached for her hand and she clung to him like a life preserver.

"It's gonna be okay," he whispered. "I'm here and he can't hurt you anymore. I promise."

Claire squeezed her eyes shut and took a deep breath. Zeke unlocked the office door and took her inside. "Wait here," he said as he left her and shut the door behind her.

"I'm so pathetic," she muttered. "How can just seeing his car make me feel so weak?"

She had a clear view of the garage from the window, but the doors were down and she couldn't see inside. Gearheads was technically not open on Saturdays. Mick liked to come in and finish up any projects he'd been working on during the week and Jeff took the towing calls for extra money. Business had been so good though, Zeke was going to have to officially open on the weekends or expand his operation. He'd been able to make all the OSHA required improvements to the shop and had even purchased some new equipment that had been on the wish list for some time. Their new website didn't advertise being open on Saturday and neither did their social media pages. So why did Brent choose to show up when he knew no one would be there?

Curiosity outweighed her fear, and Claire crept to the adjoining door… the door that would allow her to see and hear what was going on. She quietly twisted the handle and pulled the door open just a crack.

"Because you are a liar," Zeke said.

"Excuse me?" Brent coughed.

"I have proof that none of my trucks were anywhere near State Street on the day you claim one of them hit your car. Either another company is responsible or you busted the light yourself and are trying to extort me. Either way, I don't give a shit. I'm not replacing your headlight so I suggest you leave and never come back."

Claire couldn't help but grin as she watched Zeke stand up to Brent.

"You know damn well this has nothing to do with your car," Zeke added. "This is about Claire and I suggest you stay away from her or I will hurt you in ways you have yet to imagine. And I will enjoy every fucking minute of it."

Brent smiled. "You're right. This is about Claire. But you don't know her like I do and when it comes to the choice of a grease monkey or a man of stature, power and wealth like me, there will be no contest. Believe me, Mr. Gearhead," he sneered, "Claire will make the right choice. You'll see."

She flung the door open and it bounced off the wall as she stomped through to the garage. Both men were startled as she marched towards them, hands on her hips and her lips pursed. As she stood before the man that had robbed her of self-respect and filled her with shame and humiliation, she trembled… violently, but she took a deep breath and spoke with all the courage she could muster.

"How dare you?" she spat at Brent. "You have the

audacity to show up here and try to blame Zeke for something you know he didn't do? How dare you stand here and say you know me? You know nothing about me. You tried to create the woman you thought you should have and I let you. For that I will forever be sorry. I am sorry I allowed myself to be belittled and used by a shallow little man like you. You have no idea how to treat another human being, let alone a woman you professed to love. You don't know what love is," she hissed. "Love is not control. Love is not using your fist to get what you want. Love is not degradation and force," she choked. "Only cowards do that."

Brent was taken back for the fierceness of her demeanor. He'd never seen her like this. "You don't look worse for wear," he sneered.

"Not all scars can be seen, you bastard, but that doesn't mean that they don't exist," Zeke barked.

"Yeah," she noted. "I'm not that same little mouse that used to live with you, am I? If you tried to hit me now I'd beat the shit out of you, or die trying."

"No," Brent admitted. "I haven't seen you like this."

"You know what? You're right though. When it comes to the choice of a grease monkey like Zeke or a man of stature, power and wealth like you, there will be *no* contest. Zeke will win *every* time. Stature, wealth and power mean nothing if you have no character and morals to back it up. I will take *no* power and *no* wealth if it means a man like Zeke would be interested in somebody like me. And stature? You may have a position of stature in a company, but in the world of human beings you are an anthill among giants, Zeke Dayton topping that list."

Zeke's mouth dropped open. He was so full of pride for this woman he was bursting at the seams.

"I choose him!" she declared and stepped towards

Zeke and took his hand in hers. "I will choose him every day I draw breath. I choose to live my life without you in it. Now get out and don't ever come back."

Zeke squeezed her hand but kept his stare on Brent.

"Goodbye, Claire," Brent finally said and turned and walked away. "You will regret your choice one day."

"Never!" she yelled as he closed the door behind him. She stood in silence, her back perfectly straight and her eyes on the door until she heard a car start and then pull away. And then, she crumpled like a popped balloon falling to the floor. But Zeke held her. Zeke would always be by her side to hold her.

*****

"You should've seen it!" Zeke was animatedly sharing the showdown in the garage the next day over dinner at his parent's house. His parents, sisters, and brothers-in-law were all mesmerized as he told of Claire's braveness, and boldness. Claire just pushed the green beans around her plate, embarrassed they were talking about her. She didn't feel brave.

"Oh, well done!" Susan exclaimed. "Brilliantly well done!" Several others expressed the same sentiment.

"Well, then I fainted," Claire sighed.

"After he left, right?" Rebekah asked.

"Yes, after he left, thank goodness."

"Well, then," Rebekah shrugged, "you are still fabulous," she grinned. "And my hero."

"Mine too," Zeke smiled.

"So tell me," Rachel said. "How was it you were both at the shop on Saturday?"

"We'd just had brunch at the Waffle House and Zeke

needed to stop by on our way home," Claire replied as she stabbed a bean on her fork. "And Brent was there."

"I love the Waffle House!" Andy added.

"So you'd gone to breakfast together?" Rachel asked. "And then you were going *home*?"

"Yeah, we went on his motorcycle," Claire smiled.

Rachel and Rebekah exchanged glances and Zeke noticed immediately. Apparently his family were making assumptions about his and Claire's relationship. Strangely, for the first time, their assumptions were spot on.

Bill put down his knife and fork and steepled his fingers together as he leaned his elbows on the table. "Why was Brent at the shop?"

"He was trying to make Zeke pay for a broken headlight," Claire answered.

"Long story," Zeke added.

"So he knows all about our family, then?" Bill asked.

"Yeah," Zeke nodded. "But I'm assuming that's the last we'll see of him. Claire pretty much took care of that," he winked at her and she blushed.

"Alright," Rebekah said. "Spill it."

Claire looked up innocently. "What?"

"The two of you. What's going on?"

"I don't think we have to answer that," Zeke said. "It's really none of your business."

"She was my friend first," Rebekah grinned. "And then you guys got a hold of her and took her for yourselves."

"Yes," Zeke said softly. "I have. For my very own."

Just as Susan was about to scream in delight, the

doorbell rang, interrupting the celebration that was about to take place.

"Are we expecting anyone?" Bill asked.

Susan shook her head.

"I'll go," Claire offered, thrilled for a reason to escape the conversation that was embarrassing her. She walked to the front door and opened it to reveal a massive bouquet of flowers covering the holder's face. And then she saw the black Land Rover parked at the curb.

"You've gotta be freaking kidding me?" she exploded.

Within two seconds the entire family was behind her and then Bill disappeared down the hall.

"I thought I made myself very clear," Claire gulped as her back straightened.

"You did," a voice said behind the roses. "That's why I'm here… to tell you that I can change."

"Move!" Bill yelled as he pushed his way to the door, holding his rifle in both hands. "Look here you little prick. You may have been able to hurt Claire when she was under your thumb, but no more. Do you hear me? If you want to speak to her… to look at her, you'll have to go through me first!"

"And me," added Susan.

"And me," Rebekah and Rachel said in unison

Claire couldn't control her emotions as the tears poured down her cheeks. Zeke wrapped his arms her and let her wipe her nose on his shoulder.

"I'll leave this here," Brent conceded. "But may I please have a word with Claire alone? It will just take a moment and then I won't bother you anymore, Claire."

"No, you won't," bellowed Bill.

Claire took a deep breath and stepped in front of Bill. "It's okay. I'll just step outside. You have one minute Brent." She walked down the steps and onto the front lawn as Brent followed her after placing the flowers on the porch. She stayed close to the house and stood with her back to Zeke so he could watch Brent… just in case. "What do you want?" she snapped.

"I wanted to tell you something."

"Hurry up. You have exactly two minutes."

"I would have married you, you know. And I would have given you everything you ever dreamed of… everything money could buy. But you threw it away. You threw it all away." His tone was accusatory and it angered her to the bone.

"*I* threw it away? *Me*? Are you insane? Did I hit *you*? Did I break *your* finger? Did I rape *you*?"

Her voice was raised and Zeke heard every word. It killed him to stand there and not grab Brent around the neck and slowly choke the life out of him. But Susan kept her hand firmly on his arm, keeping him in place.

"Let her do this," she said. "Let her have the closure and finality she needs." So Zeke stayed put.

"That's just what happens in a relationship," Brent replied. "All I ever did was try to keep you in line. It was for your own good… to teach you how to be a good wife. Once you'd learned I would've married you."

He was teaching me? The words literally made her sick and she tasted the bile rise in the back of her throat. Her knees threatened to buckle as the so-called *lessons* he gave her flashed through her mind. She was able to compose herself long enough to say, "I want you to listen to me because I'm only going to say this once. You are no longer a part of my life. I chalk you up to a gargantuan mistake that I hope to completely forget one day. You are to stay away from me and my family," she warned.

Brent looked up at the faces glaring at him from the doorway. "You're talking about them?" he sneered. "I was your family once."

"No," she shook her head. "Family doesn't hurt each other the way you hurt me. It's done, Brent. It's over. I never want to see you again."

"You'll never be over me," he shrugged and turned and walked to his car.

As Claire hurried back to Zeke's waiting arms, her recent visit with Andy at the sheriff's office came to mind. The process of filing a restraining order against Brent had begun and the security camera footage from Agatha's house of him breaking into her apartment had been turned over for the police to investigate.

"Get off my property and don't ever come back." Bill yelled and slammed the door closed, leaving the roses outside.

"The nerve!" hissed Susan.

"He's tenacious. I'll give him that."

Rebekah glared at her husband. "You won't give him a damn thing!"

"No," Greg cowered. "I won't."

There were a few chuckles heard and then Susan said they needed to finish eating before the food got cold. "And," she added. "I think congratulations are in order," and she hugged Zeke and Claire.

The celebration, however, had to wait. Zeke escorted her to the guest room and held her in his arms while she cried. Claire needed some time to process what had just happened and to calm her nerves and settle her stomach.

Once she'd shed the final tear for her past, Zeke wiped her eyes, kissed her, and promised her that the chapter of her life that included Brent was done… finished, and she could turn the page and move forward knowing that he was merely a bad memory and would never be a part of her future.

26.

Claire stayed in her apartment on weeknights. It took a herculean effort for her not to see Zeke during the week, and he was less than thrilled with the idea, but she needed to finish out the school semester with focus. She was in two study groups and had made some great new friends. She was thoroughly enjoying her semester at school and was excelling in her classes. She attended lectures and seminars and watched webinars on her laptop in the evenings in the university library. She walked across campus confident and happy and not once looked over her shoulder, afraid of who'd she see. There was still the occasional dream that woke her in a panic but they weren't every night like they used to be, and she hoped that as time went on they would lessen with each passing week.

The other positive thing about staying in her apartment during the week was getting to know Agatha. Once a week Claire would cook dinner for two and take it upstairs to share with her landlord. At first, Agatha had grudgingly accepted Claire's offer of sharing a meal, but it only took two weeks and Agatha had offered to help, sometimes with a loaf of French bread or a green salad. Claire loved their evenings together and it was a highlight of her week. Agatha spoke of her beloved sister and some of the memories she had of teaching 8th grade English. She talked about the war and her father being drafted and stationed somewhere in the Pacific for years. She showed Claire her home and described each little knick-knack and why it was so special to her. They developed a deep friendship and Claire was almost sorry to leave after school on Fridays.

The weekends, however, were bliss on every level.

Claire and Zeke had developed a habit over the four weeks before finals started. Zeke would pick Claire up on Friday at 5:30pm on the dot. That gave her enough time to get home from her last class, pack her bag and be ready to spend three glorious nights with Zeke at his house. He had delegated locking up the office to Laura, and locking up the shop to Mick. When the sky was a brilliant blue, he'd pick her up on the motorcycle and he never got tired of seeing her squeal with delight when she'd run up the stairs and see him sitting on it waiting for her with her helmet in his hands.

Claire had come to love the motorcycle. In fact, there were many things she'd come to love since she'd met Zeke. Their favorite place to eat on Friday night was the little dive bar that had the best food in town. While waiting for their dinner, Zeke had even taught her how to play pool and darts, with Claire making plans to buy their very own pool table.

When finals were finally done and the semester was over, Zeke took her to dinner to celebrate. He drove her into the city and to a brand new restaurant that Rebekah said everyone was talking about. He'd made reservations three weeks in advance and was lucky to get a table. He'd told Claire to dress up and he asked her if she minded if they drove her car and arrived at her apartment at six sharp dressed in a black suit and pale mauve dress shirt, the top two buttons left open making him look sharp and uber sexy at the same time. She openly ogled him when she opened the door.

"Damn!" she growled. "Maybe we should just stay here instead."

"Not a chance!" he chuckled and he escorted her to her car. "I want to be seen with you. I want people to look at the two of us together and say 'How the hell did he get *her*?' And I just wanna smile like an idiot."

She laughed and handed him the keys to her car. He opened the door for her and helped her in and then dipped his head and kissed her on the cheek. "By the way," he whispered. "You look stunning… as always." And he kissed her once more and then closed the door.

Claire was dressed in new white jeans she'd found on clearance at Old Navy and her pair of Louboutins that she hadn't been able to part with. At one time they represented wealth and stature but since they had been the shoes that had carried her to her new life, they now represented freedom and love. She'd splurged on a new top – a sequined tank in jade. She wore dangly silver earrings and a silver cuff bracelet she'd found at an antique store she'd visited with Rebekah.

They drove into the city and pulled up in front of the hip restaurant and Zeke threw the keys to the valet as he escorted his girl inside. They were seated relatively quickly and a chilled bottle of expensive champagne was waiting for them.

"Are we celebrating?" Claire asked.

"We are," Zeke grinned. "You finished school!"

"Well, I still have one more semester… maybe."

"What do you mean maybe?"

"I have to figure out how to pay for it first. I'm registered and I've got my schedule but I haven't paid for it yet. I'm thinking I'm going to have to find a job."

"What do you mean a *job*?"

"So I can pay for school," Claire repeated. "I can't stop with one more semester. I *have* to finish this time."

"I agree with that," Zeke said. He nodded to the waiter who had appeared to open the champagne. The cork popped and the bubbly drink was poured into the flutes on the table.

"To you," Zeke smiled.

Claire blushed and the glasses clinked together in the air. They each took a sip and then placed their glasses on the table. "Plus, my rent is only paid for another month and then I have to pay that too."

"Eh, that's an *easy* fix," Zeke informed her.

"Oh yeah? Just not pay rent?" she laughed.

"Move in with me."

"What?" Claire choked.

"You heard me," he grinned. "I hate not being with you during the week. It kills me going to bed alone. I hate everything about the house when you're not there. It's cold and empty."

"But you lived there for years before you met me," Claire scoffed.

"I did. Only then, I had no idea what I was missing."

Claire blushed again.

"Move in with me," he pleaded. "And we can get a pool table."

That made her laugh out loud. "That's an offer I may not be able to refuse," she grinned.

"Then don't. We can play pool and make love whenever we want and you can teach me to cook and we can have breakfast in bed. I love you Claire and this has nothing to do with money. I want to be with you. This is the perfect time for you to move and I'm not sure I can take it if you say no," he grinned. "Plus," he added. "We already have an open bottle of champagne," he winked.

"You have good points, but the only one I needed to

hear was that you love me. Is tomorrow too soon?"

That night they not only celebrated at the restaurant, but also when they returned home. Passionately making love all night long, they slept in 'til noon and then headed over to Claire's apartment in Zeke's truck and loaded up all of her stuff. It didn't take too long and before she left she took her written notice up to Agatha who was genuinely sorry to see her go. She even hugged Claire and wished her well.

Back at Zeke's he helped Claire put her clothes in the closet and her make-up in the bathroom. She placed the photo she'd kept of her family on the nightstand and her mother's locket and her father's watch in the drawer. It was the only things she had left of them and though she didn't always look back with fond memories of her childhood, she loved her parents and wanted to keep the treasures to remember them.

As she looked around the bedroom, Zeke sitting on the bed smiling at her, his arms open waiting for her to come to him, she knew she was home.

*****

Birds chirping as the sun rose woke Zeke. As his eyes slowly opened a smile crept across his lips as he saw Claire sleeping soundly next to him. A week of officially living together had passed and he was confident that it had been the best week of his life. Each morning they'd made love and then showered together, making love again more often than not. Claire had made breakfast while he'd dressed for work and she's sent him off for the day with a kiss that curled his toes and made him want to turn the clocks forward so he could return to her faster. Claire had spent the first week sorting through his kitchen and tossing the items she didn't want. She'd scrubbed the bathrooms and shampooed the carpets and washed all the curtains and bedding. She said she'd love every domestic minute of it.

In the evenings she'd meet him at the door with another toe-curling kiss and then they'd either eat in if Claire had cooked, or go out to a restaurant. And each evening ended the same with them falling into bed and making love until they were spent and then fell asleep in each other's arms.

Zeke was no fool. He knew that it wouldn't always be like this. He knew the novelty would wear off and Claire would soon get tired of cleaning up after him and in a few weeks she'd be heading back to school anyway. He'd fretted over her tuition that was coming due and didn't know how to broach the subject of him paying it for her. Claire had become an independent and self-assured woman and he knew she wouldn't take kindly to anything she considered a handout. But he had a plan and it was perfect.

He continued to watch her sleep, her lips slightly apart and her chest rising with each breath. He wriggled a little, hoping the movement would wake her. He wriggled again but to no avail. Pulling on the blanket he hoped would stir her, but nothing. After several minutes of the passive approach he rolled over on top of her and smoothed the hair from her face. She smiled.

"You tease!"

Her eyes fluttered open and she giggled. "You have no idea how hard it was to pretend to still be sleeping and not laugh as you bounced all over the place."

"I was trying to be polite and let you wake up on your own," he grinned.

"Yanking the blanket from me is not being polite," she laughed. "But now that you know I'm awake, what are you going to do with me?"

He kissed her… an open-mouthed, wet, juicy kiss that had her wrapping her arms around his neck and holding him to her.

"I love you," she smiled as he broke away and took a breath.

"I love you more," he winked.

Within mere seconds they were naked and he was inside her, gasping for air as he pumped into her, her hips rising to meet him with each thrust. The friction of their bodies brought them closer and closer to climax until they reached the peak and exploded in each other's arms. Collapsing on top of her as they both fought to catch their breath, Zeke whispered into her ear.

"I didn't understand how I could want to love someone forever until you came along. You've changed my life, Claire."

She smiled and held him. She felt exactly the same way.

*****

On Monday morning Zeke asked Claire to meet him at the garage at ten. There was some business he needed her help with, to which she happily agreed.

"And maybe we could have lunch together after?" she suggested.

"Great idea."

"I'll bring a picnic," she smiled. "I haven't gone on a picnic in… well, I can't remember the last time."

"Me either," he said as he kissed the tip of her nose. "Sounds perfect."

Arriving promptly at ten o'clock, Claire left the picnic basket in the trunk of her car and casually strolled into the shop, saying hello to Mick and Jeff, and meeting the new mechanic, Randy. Then she walked into the office and chatted with Laura for a moment and then looked around for Zeke.

"He said he'd be back before ten," Laura informed her. "I guess he's running late."

The second she spoke, Zeke pulled in and jumped from his truck and raced inside. "Sorry, I'm late," he apologized and kissed Claire on the cheek. "Traffic."

"I just got here," she smiled.

"Great. Are you ready?" he asked.

"For lunch?" She was confused. "I thought we had some business to attend to."

"We do. Let's go," and he grabbed her hand and dragged her out to the truck. Then he drove for a few minutes and pulled up outside an office building.

"Where are we?" she asked.

"My lawyer's office."

"Oh, no," she choked. "Brent is really suing you?"

He chuckled. "This has absolutely nothing to do with Brent. Forget about him, k?"

"Okay," she agreed and followed him into the building. They rode the elevator to the third floor and then entered a busy law firm.

Zeke let the receptionist know they were there and within just a few minutes an older man, with little hair and a thick moustache greeted them in the lobby. They followed him back to his office where he closed the door behind them and then went and sat at his deck. "Everything is ready, just as you asked," he told Zeke.

Claire sat in the chair and wondered what in the world

was going on. She was baffled at Zeke's cheesy grin and the reason they were in a lawyer's office.

"Claire," Zeke said as he turned to her. "You have been invaluable these past few months in turning Gearheads into an extremely profitable business for me. You began the marketing for me asking nothing in return."

She began to speak but he held up his hand and silenced her.

"Let me finish," he grinned. "You worked for hours and hours setting things up and monitoring and doing all that you do every week. You've taught Laura how to use your programs and stuff and she is the happiest she's been in years, finally feeling useful and productive. I've been able to hire on a new mechanic and the financing has been approved to purchase the lot next to the shop and expand, a dream I often doubted would ever eventuate. But it has. And I owe it to you."

Again, she began to speak and this time he held a finger to her lips and "shh"ed her.

"I have offered you money countless times to pay you for all your work and you have rebuked me every time," he chuckled. "So I have come up with another way… a better way to give you the credit and the reward you deserve."

"Zeke," she smiled. This time he let her speak. "You know that I do it for you, don't you? It has nothing to do with the money or reward or recognition."

"I know that. But you're going to get it anyway," he winked. "I've made you a partner."

Her jaw dropped open and she was speechless. Zeke waited for her to say something and when she didn't he became slightly worried.

"Claire," he whispered. "Tell me what you're

thinking."

She shook her head in disbelief and looked at her hands. "I can't believe you would do that."

"Why? You are the heart and soul of everything I do. Why wouldn't I want you to be a part of Gearheads too?"

"If it's any consolation," the attorney spoke up. "I've been trying to get him to change from a sole proprietorship to a recognized legal entity for years. He has too much at stake to not be. And, there is a clause that will enable the business to pay for your college tuition since your degree is in Business Marketing."

"All you have to do is sign here," Zeke said and handed her a pen. "These lines with the arrow stickers." He pointed to the first line.

Claire held the pen in her hand and was still in shock. "Are you sure you want to do this?" she asked.

"I've never been more sure of anything. Sign it," he grinned. "Please?"

Looking down at the paper on the desk in front of her, she took a deep breath and found the line he was pointing at. As the tip of her pen touched the paper, she stopped and sat up straight. "You've put the wrong name in here," she frowned at the attorney.

"No he didn't," Zeke replied as he slid to the floor on one knee. "I told him what to put. Claire Larson Dayton. Claire? Will you be my partner? In the shop and in my life? Will you marry me? Will you be my wife?"

The attorney quietly left the room as Claire burst into tears.

"Oh, honey," Zeke soothed as he cradled her in his arms. "Don't cry. You're happy though, right?"

She nodded and sniffed and cried some more. He

chuckled softly and held her tightly until she was ready to sign the partnership papers and then he slipped the diamond ring on her finger and whispered, "Consider this your signing bonus."

*****

"I knew we'd be friends forever," Rebekah gushed as she admired Claire's ring. "And now we are going to be sisters."

"I never had siblings," Claire replied. "I couldn't have asked for a better family to marry into."

The two women hugged and then sat back and drank their coffee.

"Time to plan a wedding," Rebekah piped. "How fun!"

"I really would like it to be just the family," Claire stated. "Zeke and I agree nothing big… very intimate and nothing fancy."

"I would have thought you'd want a big wedding," Rebekah said.

"At one time I probably did," she admitted. "But that was before when I wanted a wedding and not a marriage. I understand the difference now. I want Zeke as my husband. The ceremony doesn't matter as long as the end result is us together."

"You're like a butterfly," Rebekah marveled. "When I first met you it was like you were in another world… sheltered and restricted. And then over the past few months you've undergone this dazzling transformation and you've emerged as this exquisite butterfly. I thought you were beautiful when I first met you. Actually, I was so jealous of you," she admitted with a grin. "But now, everything about you glows… you literally have this aura that is mesmerizing. You have become the most beautiful butterfly. And I couldn't have wished for a better woman for my brother to fall in love with." Rebekah had tears dripping off her chin as she spoke.

Claire couldn't hold back the tears either. They both laughed and cried and drank coffee, and then finally made a plan for the simple and elegant wedding that was fitting for Claire and Zeke.

*****

It was a glorious summer morning as Claire awoke in Zeke's arms. She could honestly say she'd never been happier. A smile spread across her face and she squeezed the man at her side, her heart overflowing with love.

She kissed his chest and inhaled his scent… sandalwood body wash and Zeke. It was her favorite smell. Carefully extricating herself from his arms, she climbed up and sat on him as his eyes slowly opened and a grin appeared.

"Good morning. How is my sexy fiancée today?" he growled as his hands gripped her hips.

"I think I'm going to be fabulous," she winked as she wriggled under his hands and felt his hardness coming to life.

"Oh yeah," he bucked as she lifted herself to accept his offer.

She rode him 'til she cried out in ecstasy as her orgasm ripped through her body. Panting she collapsed on his chest and fought for air.

"My turn," he growled as he flipped her over onto her back. There she lay with her head on the pillow, Zeke between her legs and as he entered her all she felt was pure pleasure. He drove in and out of her until she felt him stiffen and moan as he pumped his warm liquid deep into her core.

As Claire lay on the bed, Zeke's weight on top of her as he collected his breath, her mind went back to that night… that horrible night. Once again the difference was night and day. Zeke was loving and passionate and had kept his promise that his hands would only ever touch her to give her pleasure… immense pleasure. Of all the people she could have met in the gym all those months ago, she was grateful it had been Rebekah. She'd become the friend that Claire had needed and had led her to the man of her dreams… the man whom she would love for the rest of her life.

Later that morning, after Zeke had kissed her goodbye and left for work, and Claire had made the bed and loaded the dishwasher with the breakfast dishes, she drove to the florist and bought a small bouquet of flowers and went to the cemetery.

"I haven't been here for a while," she said to Greta. "But I haven't forgotten you. If anything, I think about you more now." She placed the flowers at the base of the headstone and sat on the grass.

"I wanted to tell you about Zeke," she continued. "And about the wonderful life I have. I wish with all my heart that you could have been as lucky as me. I wish that you'd had the courage to say enough is enough. I wish I could have been there to help you get out. I'm sorry I wasn't a better friend."

Claire picked at the blades of grass as she spoke. "I guess one day I snapped. I couldn't take it anymore. I'd been walking around on eggshells for so long and I finally decided not to let him hurt me again. I made a conscious choice and it's the best decision I ever made. You know, I hated P.E. in school. It was my least favorite class, and I don't think I've ever run a mile, but I did that day! I ran 'til my feet couldn't take another step, and I did it. I got away and fell in love with a man who doesn't hurt me… he loves me… truly loves me."

Claire sat at Greta's grave for several minutes as she wished that things had turned out differently for Greta. She'd read in the paper a few days earlier that Philip had been arrested for assault and had pleaded down to a misdemeanor – Assault 4 and had to pay a $500 fine. There was also 24 months of probation and Claire was happy about that. She'd wondered who he'd assaulted; they'd obviously had the guts to stand up to him and she may very well have been the first one to do it. If only it had been Greta she might still be alive. If only Claire had stood up to Brent.

"But I did," she said out loud. "I did stand up to him and look where I am because of it."

After about thirty minutes Claire stood and said her goodbyes. She climbed into her car and drove to Gearheads. She wanted to see Zeke and needed one of his warm hugs.

27.

With more 'meat on her bones,' Claire was surprised that she'd had to buy a wedding dress two sizes bigger than she was used to wearing. Zeke had assured her many times that she looked "healthy" and not to be concerned. In order to wear the designer and couture clothes from her former life, she'd had to remain a size 0 or 2, otherwise she was too big to fit into them. However, shopping at the mall, she didn't have that problem anymore.

The satin and lace strapless creation had only needed minor alterations made. The bust fit perfectly and so did the waist, but as it fell to her feet, the body-hugging gown was too long and had to be hemmed, and Claire had decided to have something blue appliqued on the bottom of her dress - a tiny butterfly. Since Rebekah had likened her to the beautiful creature, Claire had pondered on her metamorphosis from her former self to the woman she'd become. She could see a night and day difference and was proud of herself for making the necessary changes in her life that had brought her to this point. Had she stayed in the same place, she'd still be a caterpillar, allowing people to step on her and squash her. But why stay a caterpillar if you can be a butterfly?

Rachel was fussing over her hair, swept up and secured with pearl bobby pins and dotted with delicate blue flowers. Tendrils curled and framed her porcelain face and Rebekah was fixing her veil. It was time and Claire couldn't have been more ready to marry the man of her dreams. Though they'd been living together for the past several months and now worked fulltime together at Gearheads since Claire had graduated with her business marketing degree, there was something that was missing. It was the title of 'Zeke's wife' she desperately wanted.

And today she'd get it.

"It's time," Rebekah smiled. "Are you ready?"

"Oh, yes," Claire smiled. "I'm ready.

They'd found an old small church that had been converted into a reception hall. It was perfect. The old stone building and stained glass windows created the ambiance of a church but without the religious portion that Claire still had trouble accepting. There were candles on brass candelabras scattered around the room, and tiny flowers in the palest of blue accenting the roses in vases on the tables and on the end chairs of the short aisle. Only twenty or so people of their family and closest friends, Agatha included, were gathered and waiting patiently in their seats, and as Rebekah entered the hall, everyone hushed. Claire had asked her to be her matron of honor and Chloe her flower girl. Chloe was already sitting with her dad as Rebekah walked down the aisle in her off white dress with a small bouquet of roses, and then she turned and waited for Claire to follow her.

All was quiet as Claire walked through the doorway and Zeke gasped and brought his hand to his lips. He trembled as he watched her walk to him, their eyes gazing at each other as the distance between them lessened with each step.

"God, you're beautiful," he beamed as he took her hand in his. She handed the roses in her hand, tied together with a pale blue ribbon, to Rebekah and turned and faced the Dayton's pastor who would perform the ceremony.

They'd decided to write their own vows that, at the time, had seemed like a great idea. Now as Claire stood next to her love, her nerves were making her shake. She wasn't one bit nervous about marrying Zeke, just reciting the words she hoped she would be able to remember.

The pastor spoke and Claire barely heard him. As she gazed into Zeke's big brown eyes she was all but oblivious to what was happening around her. And then, it was time.

"Claire Larson," Zeke began. "You came into my life unexpectedly. I wasn't looking for love and I wasn't looking for a partner. But your beauty, inner and outer," he grinned, "captured my heart and I will love you for the rest of time. I promise before you, and our family, and God, that I will love you, and respect you, and treat you always as the princess that you are. I will honor you and worship you and our children will know without a doubt that you are and will always be the love of my life. I will care for you when you're ill and help you around the house," he grinned. "Claire you are more than my equal. You are my superior and I promise to try to deserve you every day for the rest of my life."

"How am I supposed to talk after that?" she choked as she wiped the tears through her veil. "You're messing up my make-up."

Everyone chuckled and Susan jumped up from the front row and dabbed Claire's eyes with a handkerchief, then squeezed her hands and told Claire she could do it. As she returned to her seat, Claire turned back to Zeke and took a breath.

"I wasn't looking for love when I met you either. I didn't even know what love was all about. But you, and your family, showed me what it was to be loved and they taught me how to love... how to love you. And I do, with all my heart and soul. We fit perfectly in every facet of our lives and I promise to you now, and in front of our family, that I will honor you and trust you and respect you. You are deserving of all I can give and so much more. You rescued me Zeke. You found me when I was at my lowest and lifted me up, not only giving me hope, but giving me a future. You healed my broken heart and it has mended stronger than it was before. It beats for you, and only you. You are the wind to my sails and the peanut butter to my jelly," she smiled. "I will love you forever."

Zeke wiped his eyes and smiled at the woman who had fulfilled his every need. They exchanged wedding rings, and then they were pronounced husband and wife, and their destiny was sealed. They would be each other's to love forever.

EPILOGUE

"Come to the auction with me. We can grab something to eat after," Zeke begged. "Please?"

"Fine," Claire agreed. "But why do you need me? You usually go by yourself or take one of the guys."

"I like to mix it up, Mrs. Dayton," he grinned as he grabbed her and kissed her. "Let's go." He grabbed her hand and escorted her to his truck.

The vehicle auction was something Zeke had started doing recently. There were repossessed car and trucks, occasionally a boat, and often some trade-ins that the dealership couldn't sell. On occasion there were some new cars that didn't sell and that was why Zeke was anxious to get Claire to the auction with him. Zeke had struck up a friendship with one of the auction house owners and he'd give Zeke some advance warning if there was a vehicle he thought Zeke might be interested in. Today, he was *definitely* interested in one of the cars.

Claire hung back as the crowds ogled and drooled over some of the cars but she was content to watch from a distance. When the bidding began, Zeke held her hand and was acting like it was Christmas morning.

"What's up with you?" she asked.

"You'll see."

It was the third car to be auctioned and Zeke was ready with his paddle. And then there it was.

"Happy Anniversary!" he blurted.

"What?" Their anniversary was the following day – one year of wedded bliss. The expansion of Gearheads was complete, business was booming and there were plans to open a second location. They were also in the hunt for a new home, Claire tired of the pool table having to be in the cold and dusty garage.

"We need a man cave," she'd told Zeke.

"I think those may be the sexiest words I've ever heard you utter," had been his response.

And to top off the most amazing year of her life, they'd just found out she was pregnant with a baby Dayton, due in six months. They were ecstatic and had already purchased a stroller and a crib, though both were still in boxes. And, more importantly, they'd already chosen names; Madison Greta if it was a girl, and James Ezekiel. It had definitely been a busy year.

Driven onto the floor was an Audi, an A6, red and sexy. Zeke was bouncing with excitement.

"Are you serious?" she asked.

"Don't you like it?"

"Yeah, I do. But I'm not sure this is the right time to buy a luxury car." She'd deflated him. "Come here. Let me show you something," she said as she dragged him away from the bidding war underway.

"This is the one I want."

"Are you serious?" he asked.

"Don't you like it?" She was using his words against him and was thoroughly enjoying it.

"Yeah, I do, but I wanted you to have a nice car."

"I do have a nice car," she corrected him. "It's clean and the body is in great shape and you keep it running perfectly. I don't need a new car. This is what we need to buy. Isn't it pretty?" she grinned.

Just a couple of hours later, slipping into the plush

leather seat, smelling that unique and desirable new car smell, feeling the gear shift in his hand and seeing that this vehicle had every bell and whistle imaginable was thrilling. It was beautiful and it was all theirs for a steal.

"I guess tow trucks aren't that popular today. Lucky for us," Claire giggled.

THE END

View other books by AJ Harmon at **AJHarmon.com**

If you or someone you care about is in an abusive relationship, please call 1-800-799-SAFE (7233) or visit **http://www.thehotline.org/help** to get help.

About AJ Harmon

AJ Harmon discovered her passion for writing contemporary romance novels after her children had left the nest. Born in Australia to English parents, her first loves were Pride and Prejudice, Jane Eyre and Wuthering Heights. As an adult, she still enjoys the classics but a contemporary romance novel is what she loves best. Her list of favorite authors is extensive and loves nothing more than to curl up with a great love story.

Living in Oregon with her husband and dog, her days are now spent writing the genre she loves to read and traveling around the country to signing events where she gets to meet and interact with her readers. *A Choice for Claire* is her 13th full length novel, a stand-alone, with its sequel, another stand-alone, planned for the very near future.

AJ's USA TODAY bestselling series, First Class Novels, is now in a boxed set, *First Class Family*, for readers to enjoy. Sky Romance Novels will have its' third book in the series released in 2015, *Chicago – a shot to the heart changes everything.*

Please visit AJ's website, **www.ajharmon.com** and her Facebook page, **www.facebook.com/authorAJHarmon**